TAKEN BY THE DRAGON KING

THE DRAGONS OF FIRE AND ICE

BOOK ONE

AMELIA SHAW

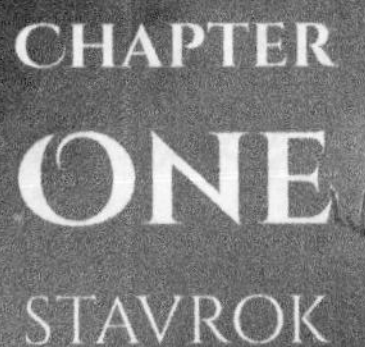

I glared at the elder standing before me. How dare he suggest something so barbaric? Sure, I hadn't found my fated mate. Sure, I was one of the only bachelor kings in our realm. But kidnap a woman from the closest human town?

He had to be fucking kidding me!

I slid my sword back into its sheath, finished with my morning training session, and handed it off to a nearby servant.

Then I narrowed my eyes at the elder. "I am your *king,* Hillsen! Do not presume to tell me what I must and must not do!" How dare he lecture me as though I was shirking my duties?

I stormed away from the elder, though I didn't want to walk away. I wanted to stay and tell him exactly where he could go.

Anger was sparking fire through my veins, and testosterone was pumping after a heavy fighting session with my training partner. I would do the old man serious bodily harm if I stayed here.

My shifter was enraged by everything going on around me. He wanted his mate as well, but the elder was suggesting I grab any woman that took my fancy—like King Magnik.

Not a chance.

Even though he was wrong about the route to my future queen, Hillsen didn't deserve to be on the wrong end of my dragon. He was, after all, only interested in the betterment of the kingdom. As was I. That had always been my focus.

But, kingdom or no kingdom, I would never stoop to mating with some random woman. Nor would I entertain what the elder had suggested: kidnap a woman to be my wife and mate, as was tradition.

My father had done it before me, and his father before him. Just because they couldn't control their shifting animal, didn't mean I would be so weak and give in to my baser urges. When I met my mate, I would woo her. Sweep her off her feet. Charm her.

I jogged over to the staircase, stepping underneath the large oil painting of my parents that hung high on the castle wall. Their faces stared down at everyone who passed through the great hall. In death as in life, they kept a faithful watch over their kingdom.

Love squeezed my heart as I remembered how caring they had been. The perfect parents, in truth, always taking care of me even when they had a whole kingdom to run.

They'd had everything a person could ask for, but... I had been their only son. Their only child and heir.

They'd left me with the crown only a handful of winters ago. Their deaths had both been accidents. That night still haunted me with all its unanswered questions.

Why had they been in the woods when the hunters had come? And why couldn't my father, the biggest of us all and the greatest fighter I'd ever known, survive the fire that broke out after he carried my mother's lifeless body back to the castle?

The courtiers whispered that he had died of a broken heart.

My parents' faces smiled down at me, golden and glowing as the sun crept in through the windows. I looked away before the bad memories could steal inside my mind and tarnish the rosy hue of my perfect memories before that terrible night.

I kept walking until I reached my bedchamber. I strode through the door and slammed it shut, still reeling with anger from my run-in.

As king, it was my duty to hear the counsel of my closest advisors—but that didn't mean I had to like what they said.

Out of nowhere, loneliness filled my gut, like an icy-cold soup.

A creak came from the huge wooden bed at the center of the room.

"Hello, my king," Daphne said, her tone seductive.

Once upon a time, she would have induced me to fall into bed with her. Not tonight though.

I sighed. My loneliness could be assuaged for an hour... a day... but not for long enough. And not by this one.

"Daphne. What are you doing here?"

She was sprawled across my bed, dressed only in her underwear, though it barely contained her ample curves.

I liked women with more flesh. Large breasts, huge ass. Something to hold during love-making and curl up against on long wintery nights.

My mate would need to be big and lush, strong enough to carry my heirs.

But this woman was not the one for me.

She pushed up onto her hands and pouted. "It's been so long, my king. Don't you crave me as you once did?"

She reached out her hand, and I was tempted by her words. Tempted to lose myself in her body. To forget my aching loneliness and the long, winding quest for my mate for a few lust-fueled hours. So far, the search for her had proven fruitless.

"No. I'm sorry Daphne. I can't."

Her wide, hopeful eyes narrowed, and her eyebrows drew together. A part of me was relieved that the savage side of her would always emerge sooner rather than later, especially when crossed.

She could be so innocent and meek in bed. When she was getting her way, that was. Deny her wishes, and you would soon see the *real* face of Daphne Montany.

Experience had taught me well in that regard.

"How can you say that to me?" she said. "We've been lovers for all our adult life. You know you want me. No one can please you as I do."

I chuckled at the arrogance in her words. She had no idea what I truly craved in the bedroom. She was a servant in my household, but nothing more.

I wanted someone who would love me, submit to me, give only to me.

Not to every man in the kingdom who looked her way.

I didn't voice these thoughts, but I let a healthy dose of irritation bleed into my tone, hoping she would get the message.

"Daphne, leave me. I need to take a shower, and if you stay, I'm afraid you'll see the rough side of my temper today."

She opened her mouth, clearly gunning for a fight. I held up my hand, letting loose the growl that had been building in my throat from the moment I'd stepped into the room.

"Daphne. I am your king. I am commanding you to leave me or face the consequences."

With a growl of frustration, she sprang up from the bed and scurried out of the room.

She knew my temper.

They *all* did.

I'd always had a stormy disposition, but the last couple of years had sent me over the edge. The loss of my parents, my lack of a mate. Most days I found it a challenge to rein in my moods, and no amount of anything—food, wine, or women—could sate my appetites for long.

I walked into the bathroom and stripped off my sweat-soaked shirt. The scent of my heat rose around me, making me groan with the need to fulfill my destiny.

To locate my mate. To fuck us both into sweet, sweet oblivion.

Maybe then I could finally find some peace.

I'd been told by my father that true happiness in the arms of your mate existed. He was the greatest king our clan had ever known. The most powerful. The most loved.

But I'd never experienced such peace for myself. Unlike my father, my mate had not been born into the local town. I couldn't smell her, despite all the nights I spent prowling down every alleyway and corner. Wherever she was, it wasn't nearby.

I'd been told, time and time over, that I would know her by sight, by taste, by smell.

I sighed. Until I found her, I had to deal with the heated dreams, the frenzies of rage, and the arousal that no number of trysts with easy women could abate.

I flicked on the hot water and walked beneath the flow, groaning out in the simple pleasure of the feeling.

I cast my mind back to Hillsen and the conversation that had interrupted my training session and had gotten me so riled up.

Aside from his bullish demands that I take a wife, there were more immediate troubles that I had to attend.

Our world was surrounded by the human world. We were enclosed, like a bubble hidden away from the eyes of ordinary souls, in a secret realm. A paranormal portal bridged the gap between us and the humans. The barrier kept us safe, and hidden, deep in the mountains of Siberia.

Our clan was one of six dragon shifter kingdoms that populated our hidden pocket of the world.

We lived in peace—most of the time. Of late, there had been rumours of an uprising, by Magnik, the king of the most southern tribe.

He had always wanted the land surrounding my castle. It was rich in rare, precious ore. We were sitting on a potential fortune if we chose to mine it and sell it to the humans beyond the portal.

But that wasn't my deal.

I avoided trading with the humans as much as possible. I didn't trust them. I'd met one, once. They were selfish. Without loyalty or bravery. It was for the best that our two worlds were separated, and we were hidden from them.

Before their death, my parents had made me vow that I would never mine the land that we'd owned for generations. It would see thousands of people lose their homes and would tear apart my kingdom.

All for the sake of money.

"Majesty. The evening guests are assembled. It's time to dress for dinner," Maddie, the housekeeper who'd looked after me since I was a child, said, stepping into the bathroom and laying out a fresh towel and my formal suit.

I groaned, venting my annoyance. "You *know* I don't like wearing that. It's too stiff."

She gave me a hard stare. Unfortunately, it was one I knew well. It told me I would do as she asked, or else.

"I know, sire. But unless you have lost your crown since we last spoke, I won't have you turning up to dinner wearing clothes fit for a farmer."

With a huff, I turned off the shower and grabbed the towel.

Maddie had been like a second mother to me since... forever. These days, with my parents gone, she barely left my side.

We'd had this argument on countless occasions.

"Who's coming tonight?" I asked. "Remind me."

"The leaders of the other five kingdoms, Majesty."

"What?"

I froze, halfway through drying my back. Had Maddie just said that *all* of the monarchs were dining here tonight?

"Since when?"

More to the point, why haven't I heard of it until now?

"Some of the elders decided to get everyone together to look over our yearly plans. The wedded monarchs are bringing their families with them."

"What?"

Four of us six were married already. Damon was the only other bachelor king and, as far as anyone could tell, he rarely stepped outside his castle.

"To make it more of an informal affair, as I understand it. Rather than an official one of state."

A growl began to rumble through my chest. With difficulty, I tamped it down.

Don't shoot the messenger, Stavrok.

"You've got to be kidding me," I said. "What do they want now?"

Maddie shrugged. "How would I know? I'm simply the maid, Your Majesty."

"Maddie, please." I crossed my arms and stared down at her, trying to maintain authority. "You know more about this kingdom than anyone. If you know why they're here, then you better tell me."

Her smile was secretive as she backed out of the bathroom. "See you downstairs, sire."

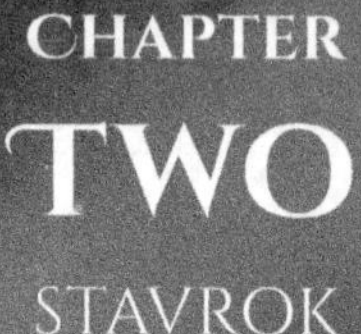

CHAPTER
TWO
STAVROK

I grabbed the suit Maddie had laid out for me and considered throwing it after her retreating form. Instead, I took a few deep breaths and pulled it on.

Was this a set up? Why was everyone conspiring against me today? This meal had to be in aid of something, but I couldn't for the life of me figure out what.

I rubbed the silk tie Maddie had laid out between finger and thumb, wrinkling my nose with distaste.

A tie as well? Shit. What am I, human?

I threw the narrow strip of material in the direction of the trash and tugged on the crisp white shirt.

Even custom made and tailored to perfection, these clothes did not sit right on me. It was expected, and befitted my position, but I never felt comfortable dressing like this.

I slicked back my long hair so that it didn't fall over my face and let out a slow exhale. I couldn't put it off any longer; it was time to make my way downstairs.

There was only one other king I got along with. Vlakid. He and I had hunted together many times. I was there when he found the woman who would be his queen. She was so beautiful that it made me sick with envy every time I saw them together. Even if she'd been a servant before he'd seen her.

As for the rest of them, well, where the night would take us was anyone's guess.

The rumble of deep male voices came from the formal dining room, and I paused before entering, gathering my strength to face them all.

Another thing my mate would make easier for me: formal gatherings.

She would be the perfect hostess, I was sure.

I craved my fated mate for more than the chance to secure my lineage. With her, I would have comfort, companionship. I wouldn't have to be the bachelor king a moment longer.

The elders and my kingdom would finally be happy with me.

I pushed open the door and everyone turned toward me. The men were standing, drinks in their hands. The women were already seated at the table.

They were all dressed as I'd been instructed to. In their royal robes. Rich fabrics topped with furs. Purples, reds and blacks. And when they looked at me, there was a mixture of jealousy and friendship written across their faces.

The men I'd known my whole life. But that was the price of power and privilege, living and knowing there were more than a few vipers in the nest.

Magnik especially. That one was a true bastard.

"Welcome." I surveyed the group before me, hands clasped behind my back. I had to look regal, self-assured. In control. "I trust your journeys were comfortable. Please, take your seats."

Delicious smells wafted through the air. The food was ready to be served. As I greeted my guests with the customary hand shaking and kisses, my stomach growled.

It had been too long since I'd last eaten.

And my dragon was hungry.

Always hungry.

I indicated the table where the women sat waiting for us. "Please. Let us eat before discussions begin."

The men around me nodded, their eyes lighting up as the servants entered, bearing platters piled high with delicacies.

A dragon shifter's hunger was ravenous all the time, especially through winter, when our metabolisms burned the hottest.

I grabbed for the cuts of stag and bear meat in front of me, loading my plate with a small mountain of food. I poured gravy over the lot and tore open the fresh, warm bread right in front of me, inhaling the steam that came from within.

I filled the bread up with meat and dipped it into a bowl of gravy before devouring the handmade sandwich in a handful of bites. My carnivorous nature really got the better of me sometimes; the dragon demanded meat, and lots of it.

I had barely slaked my hunger by the time Barrick called out to me from the other end of the table.

"Stavrok! I heard your elders are pushing you to enter the human realm to find your mate." He grunted, showing his disgust. "Are you willing to taint the pure blood of your dragon so easily?"

Barrick was the oldest of us, closer to fifty than forty. He was thinner and smaller, with long black hair that reminded me of a crow.

I shot a glare at him and picked up my wine glass, downing the thick red liquor and preparing my answer carefully. Though I agreed with him, that the mixing of my blood with a human would weaken my offspring, I wasn't going to give him the satisfaction of knowing that.

It was vital to show strength when conversing with another king. I took the remark for the challenge it was, and I knew I had to parry the blow with one of my own.

"I'm not going to grab the first woman who climbs into my

bed, Barrick." I let my gaze wander over to the woman by his side. A peasant. His wife. Pregnant for the third time. Or was it the fourth?

I raised an eyebrow and watched as Barrick's face coloured with heat.

"You neglect the continuation of your bloodline, Stavrok," he said. "Your heirs. Without a son, your kingdom is weak, vulnerable."

I laughed aloud. "Vulnerable? I am not weak, and neither is my kingdom. I will find my true mate, no matter how long I have to wait."

I looked around the room at the five kings and four of their queens. Together, we ruled the kingdoms of *Fire and Ice.*

It wasn't the official name of our hidden country, but it was a name I'd given to my snowy lands a long time ago, when I was a child, and it had stuck.

"That may be a mistake, my friend. You're not getting any younger," Vlakid said to my right.

I glared at him, but there was no real heat behind the look. Vlakid was too relaxed to be a king, too kind. He had never been anything other than a firm friend and ally.

"Just because you found your mate working as a laundress in your town, Vlakid..." I gave his beautiful wife a smile, then shifted my gaze back to my friend. "You think such fortune will fall to everyone around you. Some of us aren't so lucky."

I'd scoured the city, and the surrounding towns. All the married kings in the room had found their wives practically on their doorstep, in their own hometowns, or thereabouts.

Everyone except for Damon and myself.

Mine had either never been born, died early, or she was yet to reach maturity. All of those possibilities were devastating and frustrating in the extreme. The worst part was, I simply didn't know.

A servant stepped forward and re-filled my glass. I reached for my wine and glanced down the table to Damon, the stoic quiet king who was also queen-less. He met my gaze and inclined his head in a silent moment of respect.

Marienne, Magnik's queen on the other side of me, reached out and touched my hand. Her long fingers were elegant, just like the rest of her, but the touch was brief as if she feared I might lash out at her forwardness. "Would you allow me the honor of reading your palm, King Stavrok?"

I moved my hand further away from her, feeling her subtle magic reach out after me like a shimmer across a pool.

"Readings?" My gaze snapped to her husband. "Is that why your kingdom has grown so prosperous of late, Magnik?"

He merely shrugged. "My wife has many talents," he said, a lecherous smile lifting his lips, "and she advises us regarding the weather and our crops. As she should. It is her duty and it benefits our people."

I gave him a knowing stare before sliding my gaze to Marienne. I was certain she helped with more than that. Magnik had renovated his palace in the past year and his clothes and jewels had multiplied in number. Their kingdom was more powerful than ever.

Perhaps she was predicting shifts in the humans' economy? The stock exchange, maybe. The practices weren't technically forbidden, but it was frowned upon to make money on the humans in such a way. Especially when Magnik had married a sorceress. It was the very definition of cheating.

Marienne was looking more tired than I'd ever seen her, with dark circles beneath her eyes. Did Magnik treat her well? As I pondered their relationship, she said to me again. "Stavrok. I implore you to let me help you. I may be able to tell you where to look."

Her purple irises whirled like rockpools, betraying some kind of emotion that I couldn't read.

"Why would you want to help me, Mari?"

She gave me a gentle smile that seemed genuine. "Because you are a good and kind man. And your dragon is growing impatient. I can feel him stirring. You will not be able to control him much longer."

I opened my mouth to tell her she was wrong. Not about her character assessment, but about the strength of my will against my dragon's restlessness. I had been fighting him all my life. But the heat of my dragon was stronger in my blood now. I could feel it flowing and shifting, ever impatient under my skin.

It was just as she said, though I wouldn't admit it out loud to anyone, even on my deathbed.

I relented, gritting the words out before I could rethink them. "Fine. Tell me. Where is she?"

She bit her lip. "I don't know yet. My magic isn't as strong as I would like at present. But if you'd let me hold both of your hands for a moment, the connection might help. I can try to give you the answers you seek."

A chuckle rose in my throat.

The sorceress wants me to let her inside my mind, does she?

Not a chance.

"Thank you for your offer, but I'm afraid I'll have to decline."

She sank back in her seat, her shoulders slumping a little as if my answer dejected her.

I turned away from her and focused my attention on Vlakid, who threw me an easy smile and started telling me about his youngest child, a baby girl born over the last winter.

Even in this den of powerful sovereign rulers, I had friends. People I could count on to turn my mind onto happier things.

After that exchange with Queen Marienne, I forced the conversation to politics, to trade and councils. After all, that was the purpose of our gathering. But I couldn't ignore Marienne's intent gaze upon me throughout the remainder of the meal. I sensed she was measuring me, weighing her options.

I wasn't convinced that her offer of help came solely from the goodness of her heart.

Witches and mages in our kingdoms regularly foretold the future, but such services always came with a price. Although Marienne was a queen by marriage, with all the wealth of her husband's kingdom already at her beck and call, I was concerned the payment she would require for this information would be more than I would willingly give.

We finished dinner, and to my relief, the subject of my future wife didn't come up again. In fact, everyone seemed to be steering clear of the topic entirely.

Perhaps they were fearful my temper might get the better of me.

It was infuriating to be the object of such speculation, but I knew it wouldn't end until I found my mate.

Why didn't they pester the solemn, quiet Damon? With his golden hair and bright blue eyes, it was a mystery why he was unmarried. And why he never spoke.

We moved into the grand hallway. My guests glittered in their finery; the women's skirts swirled in the candlelight, and the children ran in and out of their parents' legs, shrieking with the excitement of staying up so late.

I wished they would all leave. A pressure was starting to build behind my eyes. I just wanted to be somewhere else, alone. Preferably in a dark room.

Queen Marienne strolled up to me, unspeaking. What did she want? Surely not to offer me guidance once again about my mate. Her foot caught on a crooked flagstone. As she fell, crying out, I grabbed her hands to steady her.

I realized my error moments too late.

Her hands clasped mine, holding tight, and electricity shot through my palms as her magic and my dragon wove together.

Her head snapped up and our gazes locked onto each other.

I saw what she saw; it raced from her mind to my heart and back again, flowing in an unstoppable current that pooled together, forming a clear image that was almost vivid enough to reach out and touch.

It hit me like a thunderbolt.

My mate was a human. Alive, and whole, and beautiful. And entirely unaware of my presence, over all these years. She was just waiting to be found. Across the magical void that kept her land separate from mine.

THREE

STAVROK

A gasp filled my throat, making it feel as though a hand squeezed tight around my heart. The shock of the realization pounded through my brain, over and over.

My mate. That was my mate!

Or was it? What, exactly, had I seen? A picture Marienne had possibly forced into my mind on behalf of her husband? A cunning deception intended to destabilize a rival king?

Or was that image the truth?

I dragged Marienne to her feet, and she came up, trembling. Her husband materialized beside her, pulling her from me so quickly she stumbled backward and almost fell once again.

The moment her connection with me was broken, my mind cleared and all the feelings about the woman who was to be my queen, my fated mate, were gone.

"Stop that, Marienne. You're embarrassing me." Magnik hissed at her, and Marienne instantly flinched as though expecting him to strike her.

I frowned at the exchange, not enjoying see anyone flinch away from a loved one. I'd heard rumors over the years that Marienne and Magnik's marriage was not a happy one. She had no children, and it was clear he had chosen her for her powers, not for love. Had those rumors been true? And worse, did he raise his hand to her on occasion?

"I need to help him." She whispered the words in Magnik's direction but he was already storming away in a rage.

I narrowed my eyes again. If this was a deception, they didn't seem to be on it together.

"Did you see her?" Queen Marienne asked me, her strange, ethereal eyes wide. She sounded part-enthralled, part-fearful.

I stared at her, my arms twitching with a strange sort of energy. I could feel my shifter inside my chest, stretching, his wings unfurling. Ready for flight.

Damn. This was *not* the time to lose control.

"Did you put that vision inside my head, Marienne?" I demanded. It was a struggle to keep my voice steady.

She shook her head vehemently, purple magic swirling intensely behind her eyes. "No! I *told* you that if you would spare me a moment, I could try and help you find your mate."

I shivered and clenched my muscles, drawing my shoulder blades together in a fruitless attempt to control my dragon.

"That woman was my mate? Are you sure?" I asked, urgency growing in my tone.

I wouldn't be able to speak soon and I needed to know if what I saw was real.

Echoes of the vision flickered through my mind: a blonde woman, with hair that flowed and shone in the sunlight, curling all the way down to the small of her back. Her eyes were a brilliant emerald green, like the stones we mined from the caves near our home.

She had a fire about her, a vivacious energy that was a rarity in a human.

"Yes, I'm sure. I don't control my magic, King Stavrok," Marienne said, spreading out her hands in a supplicating manner. "The vision was a gift."

I stiffened against the word. "A gift I did not ask for, Mari, and you should not ask for payment."

Her eyes met mine. Her gaze was as unreadable as ever, but I could detect a shadow of hurt and frustration in her expression.

"Stavrok, your friendship alone is payment enough. We are to rule our kingdoms alongside one another for the rest of our lives, are we not? Let us try to be friends."

She turned away, as if not expecting an answer, and glided back across the room to Magnik's side. When she reached him, her husband turned his back on her and filled his goblet with wine once again.

I could almost see the defeat in Marienne's posture and, for a moment, my heart went out to the woman. But I had no time to dwell on the state of another's marriage.

I could see my mate so clearly in my mind. My dragon wanted to hunt for her, shake free. Leave the castle this very night.

Did I dare?

"Marienne?" I called after her, quickly crossing the room and closing the gap. "Tell me, what more do you know? Where should I look for her?"

The queen whirled and faced me squarely. "You must let me complete your reading if you want to know everything, Stavrok."

Damn. I didn't have much of a choice. She had me pressed into a corner. I wanted to know who my mate was, and where I could find her.

"No payment required," she added wryly.

"Very well."

It was a dangerous gamble.

If she probed too hard in my mind and found out too much about my kingdom, it could tip the balance of our world too far in her husband's favor. The six clans relied on a mutual fear and respect of the other kingdoms, and we kept our secrets closely guarded.

If I wanted answers, I had no choice.

Extending both of my hands, I kept my expression steely. Before she could take hold, I drew back. "Marienne. My mind is my own. Do not rifle through my thoughts. Tell me only what I want to know."

"I give you my word, Stavrok." She granted me a short nod, and I allowed her to clasp my hands.

Her gaze snapped to mine. This time, I willingly surrendered to her power.

Our eyes clashed and a myriad of images flashed across my mind as I struggled to keep calm and not fight against the jolts of electricity coursing through my veins.

I saw an image of the woman flowing through my mind again. She was with a child—no, with many children—laughing with them, helping them paint with their fingers on a giant sheet of paper.

Human children...

Then the picture changed. It was the same woman, sitting with an older couple on their front porch, clutching steaming mugs of coffee and talking quietly.

The images came faster, forming and reforming in front of my eyes. Now she was asleep, spread out in the middle of a large four-poster bed, alone. Her long golden hair was pale in the moonlight, fanned out over the pillow, and her arms were curved upwards, elongating her torso.

Her eyelashes brushed her cheeks, hiding her bright eyes. I watched her chest rise and fall, my eyes tracing over her full breasts and her long, pale throat...

I broke away, gasping for breath, unable to handle the force of my wanting for another minute.

My heart ached for the woman who would fulfill me.

And damn it all... she's human!

"Did you get enough? Do you know how to find her?" I panted as I spoke, my heart thundering as though I'd run up a thousand steps to the highest turret in the castle.

Marienne nodded, staggering backward. Her lips were pale, and her frame seemed smaller somehow.

Drained of energy, I guessed.

Her husband turned to watch our exchange, a snarl on his face as his wife stumbled then caught herself against a chair. He didn't step forward to help her.

I did, feeling the need to extend my arm and offer her the support she so obviously needed. That wasn't my place. It should have been Magnik's.

"She's human?" I asked, gently this time. I needed to confirm I'd gotten that part right, at least.

"Yes, she belongs to the human realm. But..."

I tilted my head, confused by the caveat. "But what?"

Marienne frowned, fiddling with the rings that studded her slender fingers. "I sense some magic in her. It's possible that one of our ancestors ventured out and bred with a human in that area a long time ago. I can't be sure. What I do know is, she is yours, Stavrok. Your fated mate. And she isn't far away. She lives in the first town past the border. You'll know her on sight."

The last thing I wanted was to head out there. I didn't trust the human race. But what choice did I have? Fate knew best. If she was my mate, surely there would be good in her.

I swallowed down the bile that rose. "Are the old stories true? Will my dragon kidnap her when he sees her?"

A small smile rose on Queen Marienne's face. "What's wrong, Stavrok? Never met a woman who didn't dive into your bed the moment you set eyes on her? Apart from me, of course."

I gave her a wry smile. "No, I haven't, actually."

My pride balked at the idea of kidnapping *anyone*, let alone the woman who I would make my queen, the mother of my children.

As Marienne had pointed out, I'd never wanted for willing women in my bed. As the king, every courtier all the way down to the lowliest townsperson wanted my favor. I was generous with bestowing it. As a virile man, I could have one, two, even three in a night without tiring.

"My father once told me that a true fated mate would not fall for me on sight. She would need to be taken and brought here, and only then would our bond be sealed."

The whole concept irked me. Why the hell would I force a woman into my bed who didn't want to be there?

Marienne shrugged her slender shoulders. "I can't help you any further, Stavrok. Your dragon will know what to do when the time comes."

She turned to her husband and I saw her recoil. Why... I wasn't sure. "Come, my king. Let us return home. I fear I have overexerted myself."

"Then go sit down, before you fall down," Magnik snapped. "And you will wait for me. I am not ready to return home yet."

I saw it again; the strain in her body, the faint lines that had appeared at the corners of her eyes and around the edges of her mouth. How much did it cost the sorceress to call upon her magic in such a way?

She pulled out a chair and sat upon it, and I saw her fighting to keep her posture straight.

"Mari," I said, feeling pity when I looked at her weary form. "I thank you."

She threw me a small smile. "Go, Stavrok. Fly there now. I know you need to. Don't hold out against it any longer."

My gaze went to the window on my right. It was huge and ancient, and bolted heavily. Its diamond-patterned glass winked at me, as if in invitation.

I couldn't, not now. It was pitch dark outside, and heavy snow tumbled from the skies above. The idea was absurd, surely…

"Sire, please." Hillsen's voice interrupted my reverie. The elder who had advised my father on many important decisions now advised me, and it seemed he had gleaned the current direction of my thoughts. "The council and I are in complete agreement. Surely you must see our point. As the only unmarried king you must…"

I put up my hand, silencing Hillsen.

"I quite agree, Hillsen. I will not return without a queen."

I unbolted the large window and pushed it open. The castle was built high up on the mountainside.

Cold blustery air blew in and snow landed on my overheated skin. I was glad for the relief of it, but the flakes melted as soon as they touched my flesh. I was as hot as a furnace, but exposure to the elements wouldn't be enough. Only one thing could sate the fire within.

I'd made my decision. I stripped off my coat jacket and tossed it to the floor. My shirt and my pants followed.

"My king, this is not advisable. Where are you going?"

I looked at the elder and raised a brow. "I told you, Hillsen. I need to find my queen. I will return home before the sun sets tomorrow."

Now completely unclothed, I stepped up onto the ledge and called to my dragon.

He wasn't far away. He had been under the surface of my skin for hours now, through the whole evening. Circling inside of me, impatient. Ready and waiting for my shift.

I dove out the window. The cold air whipped around my body as I plummeted through the snowfall toward the jagged rocks below.

My dragon jumped forward and my body transformed into an

animal designed to cut through the air like a blade through silk. A creature of flight, huge and majestic.

My skin rippled, and my scales emerged. My toes curled into claws. Wings sprouted from my shoulder blades, stretching wide and catching the undercurrent of air in a heartbeat.

And, with that, I was soaring, skimming along the ground before shooting up and over the castle in a wide arc.

Fire lit up my throat and there was a heavy ache in my heart. I needed to find my mate, my queen. The woman who was born to complete me.

The one who would rule my kingdom by my side and provide me with my heirs, secure my dynasty for generations to come.

Children. Baby dragons. Hopefully... if a human could breed with a man such as me.

There was only one way to tell. And that was to do what my father had always said I would do, and what I always hoped to avoid.

I must find my mate and bring her back home with me, taking her away from her world and everything she held dear.

My wings carried me toward the border that connected the human world to ours.

I closed my eyes as I hit the invisible barrier. A cold shudder passed over my scales as I emerged through the other side.

It was warmer in the human world. As I sank down and flew close to the ground, it occurred to me that these people were not used to seeing dragons flying around in their airspace.

The last thing I needed was to collide with a passing aeroplane.

My feet hit the ground, as I shifted back to my human self. The transition was smooth and steady despite my agitated state.

My skin burned against the night air, and I looked around, wondering where I would be able to find clothes at this hour.

The most inconvenient part of shifting was not being able to carry clothes with me. Not that I worried much when I travelled in our world. Everyone knew who I was, and my noble standing ensured that they would come running with robes to cover my nakedness.

It was slightly humiliating to stand out here with no one around.

I walked through the woods, trudging along until I came upon a ploughed field. At the edge of it stood a small farmhouse with a flagpole in the front yard. The flag fluttered in the wind, and even from this distance I could make out a large red dragon emblazoned on it.

Happiness lit up my heart.

I knew that sign. It appeared that a tiny piece of my world had crept into theirs.

These people would help me.

I strode across the field and thumped several times on the door, covering myself the best I could with my hands. I was thankful that it was dark, at least.

After a few minutes, a man emerged. He took one look at me and called back into the house.

"Joanie! We have a visitor."

He opened the door wider and grabbed for a large fur great-coat that hung in the entrance hall. "Here, take this. You'd better come in."

I had to duck my head through the low doorway. I wrapped myself in the coat and glanced around. It was a comfortable home with humble furnishings. A fire roared in the hearth, and I gravitated toward it.

"Thank you," I said, turning back to him. "For your hospitality."

The man gave me a tight smile. His gaze roamed up and down my body as though he'd never seen a dragon shifter before. Which didn't make sense. They had the flag flying and had welcomed me inside.

We were slightly different to humans. Far taller on average, and broader with it. My tattoos indicated my royal blood—not that these two people would know it.

A woman came into the hallway, carrying a steaming mug. Her eyes widened when she saw me.

Then her gaze dropped. "You're a Dragon *King.*"

Her husband blinked, staring at me. Slowly, he began to back away.

I lifted up my head. "How did you know?"

I knotted the tie around the coat and took the cup of hot drink the woman handed to me.

"I recognise your chest tattoo." She motioned to it, giving a shaky laugh. "My mother taught me all of the Royal Heraldic symbols in case I ever met one of your kind."

I nodded before taking a sip of the bitter drink. I couldn't complain, though. It spread much needed warmth through my belly. I turned my head toward the fire, staring into the flames.

"Your mother knew of our ways?" I asked.

The woman took a seat in the armchair beside the fire, motioning me to sit on the loveseat opposite. I sank into it and barely fit. The seat was tiny, made for humans.

"Yes. She was born in Jerriak, but she settled here with my father many years ago. We are the gatekeepers, Majesty. I have been charged with the responsibility of helping anyone who crosses the border."

I hadn't known such people existed until now. I was grateful for them; my kind had a friendly face to turn to when they entered this realm.

I set my cup down on a nearby coffee table that looked hand made. I leaned forward. "On behalf of my people, I thank you, madam. I shall need some clothes, though I'm afraid I don't have any coin with me."

My impromptu visit seemed more ridiculous with each passing moment. I hadn't brought clothes or money, and I had no plan that extended beyond making it to the human world.

I'd simply followed my instincts and the words of a witch.

Not one of my smarter moves, truth be told.

"Oh, that's no problem, sire," she said.

"Stavrok."

She got to her feet with a smile. "King Stavrok. Please, come this way. We have lots of clothes in storage, although I have to admit, you're bigger than most of the men we've seen cross the border."

I inclined my head at the awkward compliment.

Aside from the clear difference between me and human men, I was taller and broader than most of my kinsmen. Being of royal blood, and a man with a desire to be the fittest warrior I could be, I was unusually large.

I stood up, grateful to be out of the clutches of the loveseat. "Thank you. Anything you have will be appreciated."

The woman led me into a spare bedroom with a single small bed, then pointed to a huge closet. "In here," she said.

She opened the doors to the closet and revealed the contents. It was filled with clothes for every sort of person who may visit them. Winter dresses with long sleeves. Jackets and long coats. Shirts and pants. I wondered how long she had been helping people cross the border. My kingdom owed her a great debt it appeared.

And even more so, it seemed that I was wrong in my assumption that all humans were selfish creatures. There was a woman in front of me who came from a line of people who looked after my kind. I had to hope that my mate would be of the same ilk.

I grabbed some thick pants, a long-sleeved shirt, and a sweater. Simple human fare. If the clothes survived the journey home, I suspected Maddie would be most displeased to see me in such attire.

Once I was dressed, we walked back into the living room to re-join the woman's husband.

I turned to them. "Can I ask, how often do you see my kind pass through from the border?"

I'd had no idea that humans even knew about us. Perhaps I was more out of touch with my kingdom than I'd realized.

"Not often." She shrugged. "Maybe once or twice a month."

"A month?" I struggled to keep my voice level.

That was so much more than I'd anticipated.

I needed to investigate this further. Were people so unhappy in the kingdom they would abandon it for this strange land? Or did they only visit for a short while, then return? Did they want for things that our world couldn't provide? Whatever it was, it couldn't stand. I cared for my people, and they cared for me in return.

But those were considerations for another day. I had a big enough task ahead of me this night.

"I'm looking for a woman," I said. "I need to get into the closest town as soon as possible."

"Of course. We'll help in any way we can," the woman said. "Do you know her name, or where she works?"

I shook my head. "I know nothing, except what she looks like, and that she may have children. Or else, she cares for them in some capacity. It wasn't clear... I'm afraid the manner of her discovery was... unusual." I paused. "It's essential that I find her."

The couple glanced at each other. The woman gestured that I should follow them back into the living area.

I went with them. The man stoked the fire in the grate, his back toward me. I sensed his tension; my kind made human men nervous. Something in their biology saw us as a threat.

The woman walked out of the room and returned with a plate of food, fit for a common man.

"Forgive me, sire. We don't have anything special..."

I smiled and took a cake that she offered. "This is perfect."

We sat and they turned to me.

The woman leaned forward. "Perhaps if you described the woman, we might be able to help."

"She has bright emerald green eyes, and long blonde hair. She is striking, and strong, and though I haven't met her, I believe she will have a temper that could shake the foundations of this house."

The woman's eyes went wide.

"We, uh, know of such a woman. She lives in the next town over. She's quite famous around these parts."

"For what?" I ask, fear sinking into my gut.

Please, don't say that she is the town whore. I couldn't bear it.

"Well, for one thing, her striking looks." The woman furrowed her brow, staring into the roaring fireplace. "And for the other, turning down every guy that asks her out. She's had plenty of offers, I can tell you that much."

My heart leapt, threatening to burst out of my chest. That sounded like the beauty I'd seen in Marienne's vision.

"I must go to her, immediately. Do you know where she lives?"

The couple shared a look.

"Yes," the woman replied. "A few blocks over from the day-care center she works at. But she will be asleep now, so it may be better if you stop here for the night. We can take you to her in the morning. It's no trouble."

The idea didn't sit right with me. I looked at the clock. Yes, it was almost midnight, far past the time that humans typically went to bed.

Now that I knew her location, I could practically feel her presence. She was so close. Even sitting here was proving difficult. My urges were like an ever-present itch under my skin, and I needed to take care of them before my dragon took control.

"Thank you for your concern." I lowered my eyes, trying not to fidget in my impatience. It was unbecoming for a king. "I'm afraid there is a possibility I may shift when I meet her. It is best I go now, while the cloak of darkness can cover me."

I stood up, unsure whether I should have explained so much to complete strangers. And humans, at that.

Still, they'd provided me with warm clothing, shelter, and food. My trust in them hadn't been misplaced so far.

They got to their feet. The man seemed hesitant, but the woman carried a look of determination on her face that reminded me of Maddie.

"We will help you, King Stavrok," she said, drawing herself up to her full, if diminutive, height. "I'd consider it an honor."

"I'll get the keys to the truck," her husband said, before heading through a low doorway at the back of the room.

"You're sure you know where she lives?" I asked the woman.

I *had* to be sure. I had left too much of this excursion to chance already, and I couldn't afford to linger long in the human world.

The woman pulled on a winter jacket. "Yes, we do. My mother told me stories about her lands when I was a child. Is she your mate, sire?"

Technically I wouldn't know until my dragon sensed her. But I had hope.

"I have been told that she is," I said, my voice soft. "But I cannot tell until I meet her in person. So, we both shall see soon enough."

We headed outside to a large truck. It was a huge, rusty thing, older than me by the look of it. Hopefully, it would transport me to where we needed to go.

If it couldn't, I would walk. A hundred miles, if I had to.

Nothing, in this world or the next, was stopping me from meeting the woman who could be the mate I'd dreamed about for so long.

The dream was back, swirling around me in the darkness. I had dreamt the same dream for as long as I could remember. Over the years, it came and went, sometimes plaguing me for months on end, then disappearing for a time before returning, more vivid than ever.

It was always the same. I dreamed of a world of Fire and Ice, a dark, howling storm where the elements tore through my hair and clothes. The wind would whip around my form while I shivered, fear and awe rooting me to the spot.

At the center of it all was a man, standing on the clifftop. Thunderclaps shook the sky above his strong frame, and lighting flashed across his harsh features. He belonged in this hazardous world. He wasn't afraid of anything.

He held my gaze, unmoved by the chaos around him. He never spoke, but I knew that he was calling to me.

And I knew that I would go to him.

A bolt of lightning split the sky in two, and I screamed as the world darkened and my vision was obscured by a pair of huge, leathery wings.

I shuddered, crying out as my subconscious clawed its way back to reality.

Panting hard against the fear racing along my veins, I managed to struggle onto my elbows and pull myself into an upright position in bed.

What had woken me?

Surely not the dreams. I'd accepted them as a matter of course long ago.

A loud and persistent knocking came from downstairs. Someone was hammering on my front door like they were going to break it open.

I froze.

The clock told me it was just past midnight.

I relaxed back into the pillows with a huff. Who on *earth* would be knocking on my door in the middle of the night? On a Tuesday, no less?

Talk about rude.

I closed my eyes and prayed they would go away. Whatever it was, I would deal with it in the morning. I had an early start and a bunch of rowdy kids to manage tomorrow.

"Lucy! Open the door! *Lucy!*"

The call was loud and insistent, but I didn't recognise the voice. I groaned as I pushed back my thick, warm duvet and fumbled in the dark for my dressing gown.

There better be a major emergency to be disturbing my sleep like this. The noise was sure to wake the neighbours, which was the last thing I needed.

I shoved my feet into my slippers, cursing under my breath, and padded downstairs.

A glance through the spy hole told me my visitors were an elderly couple I knew vaguely by sight. I was more confused than ever. Both by their presence and the fact that they apparently knew where I lived.

I pulled open the door, trying to quell the worry that seeped through my chest.

I drew my robe tight around me, shivering at the blast of cold night air. "Can I help you?"

They moved apart, revealing a third figure in the group, standing in the darkness behind them. He was huge in stature, dwarfing the man and woman on either side of him. He stepped forward; his eyes fixed on mine.

I knew him.

I *knew* him. In the marrow of my bones. I felt a shiver pass through my body, and my breath caught in my throat.

"Who are you?" My voice came out as a shaky whisper.

He was the man who had haunted my dreams all these years. The recognition shocked me to the core. This figment of my imagination appearing on my doorstep in the dead of night... It was like falling under a spell.

Those eyes. Those silver-gray eyes. Glowing, lighting me up from within.

Calling to me.

The man moved as if to step into my house, and I held up a hand in warning.

"Don't come any further. You are not welcome in my house."

Despite my words, my body was overtaken by a sensation I'd never experienced before. I ached, throbbed, lusted for this giant of a man. My body curved toward his without my permission as I stared up at him.

He towered above me. His shoulders spanned the width of my doorway. He was the biggest man I'd ever met in my life. His thigh muscles bulged through the thick pants encasing them in a way that made my mouth dry.

Despite the anger in my gut that roared like a fire in the dead of winter, honey melted in my core. A sure sign of a pure lust. I'd been turned on before, but not like this.

This was… different.

This was *terrifying.*

"Stop. Seriously!" I put up my hands to try and halt him as he moved into my house.

The look in his eyes was strange. It was almost like he hadn't registered my defiance at all.

I backed up and pressed my hands into his chest, glaring at him with all my might.

My hidden desires, my carnal needs, spiralled up inside of me and my hands clung tight to his sweater. I stared at his mouth and knew, deep within my soul, that this man was meant to be mine.

No!

It was impossible. This was a stranger. I should be quaking with fear right now, not flushed and heated with desire. I especially shouldn't be raking my hands over his chest because I couldn't decide whether to push him back or pull him closer.

"You're coming with me," he said.

He bent down and lifted me up like I weighed nothing at all. The world tilted. I shrieked with rage, hammering my fists against his rock-hard ass as he marched outside into the cold with me over his shoulder.

"Put. Me. Down!"

As soon as I spoke, my feet hit the earth and I swayed, feeling the ground move under me. I staggered a little before regaining my footing.

The man in front of me was shaking. With rage? With desire?

"Get back. He's going to shift, and you need to get out of the way."

The woman who'd knocked on my door hooked a hand around my elbow and yanked me back. My breath caught in my throat as I watched, stricken.

Before me, the man began to glow.

An unreal shimmer of light encased his body. Suddenly, he changed.

He grew even bigger, his clothes ripping and shredding as a beast emerged from the man who'd once stood in his place.

"It's a... It's a..." I couldn't say it.

My heart burst into song and started pounding against my chest. Every part of me should be terrified of the creature looming over me, but I couldn't run. Couldn't hide. I could only stare at the magnificence before me.

"It's a dragon," the woman behind me whispered.

I dragged my gaze away to look at the couple surrounding me.

They stared at the mythical creature, awe shining in their eyes, like they were witnessing a miracle.

How were they not frightened?

Adrenaline zinged through my veins at a million miles an hour.

I twisted in the woman's grasp, managing to break away from her and stumble back a couple of paces.

"We have to get out of here!" I yelled.

"Don't run!" she said as I edged back toward my house. "Don't go back inside, Lucy. He'll destroy your house to get to you if he has to!"

At that, I froze.

I'd worked day and night for years to afford the deposit for this house. I wasn't letting some man... dragon... *thing*... destroy it right in front of my eyes.

"What does it want?" I yelled at her.

The sound of the dragon's ragged breathing was as noisy as a storm blowing through the trees around my house.

The woman turned toward me, and a strange smile tilted up her features.

"He wants you, Lucy. You'll have to go with him."

I didn't even hesitate in my answer. "No fucking way."

Dragon-clawed hands lifted me, holding me firm against the cold scales of his belly and chest. The grip of the dragon was strong, and the more I struggled, the tighter the hold became.

"Help!" I screamed, thrashing against my restraints.

It was absolutely no use. The clawed arms held me effortlessly, securing me as if I weighed no more than a sack of grain.

For a creature this size, I probably did.

My confusion and rage began to ebb away, and fear rippled through my body.

A cold sweat beaded at the back on my neck, and I shivered. The erratic pulse of my heart thundered in my chest, making my head spin.

This has to be a dream! Surely? There was no other rational explanation.

As soon as I'd had the thought, my breathing settled as I began to calm down.

Of course. Now it made sense. Trust *me* to dream up something this ludicrous.

I plummeted toward the earth as the great beast crouched down. I shrieked, pushing at its toes that held me firm. Then the dragon launched up, into the air with one powerful push of its wings.

My stomach lurched and I cried out. I heard a hysterical peal of laughter as the snow and cold wind blasted my face. It took me a second to realise the sound had come from me.

I had to wake up. This was totally insane.

"Wake up. Wake up. Wake up," I muttered to myself.

Beneath us, the ground flew past my eyes at a dizzying pace, spiralling and shrinking, familiar landmarks growing smaller and smaller as we climbed through the air.

Once we reached an altitude that made me dizzy, the dragon stopped flapping his wings and began to soar through the air.

Then suddenly, we struck against something. It was an invisible forcefield of some sort, a barrier I couldn't see, but I felt the shift in the air as we passed through it.

I whipped my head around, trying to get a good look at it, but all I could make out was swirling darkness behind us.

I gasped and trembled, gazing down at the landscape below.

I was in a different world now. Below us stood craggy, snow-topped mountains. I glanced ahead and there in the distance stood an ancient castle, nestled amongst more mountains.

We flew over a dense, dark forest and off in the distance there were dark, soaring shapes in the black sky. *Oh my God.* They were riding the currents of air, spiraling through the heavens before swooping down into deep ravines. In the far distance, there were echoes of an unearthly roar.

More dragons.

I whimpered. "Wake up, Lucy. You have *got* to wake up."

This couldn't be real.

Maybe if I refused to accept what I was seeing, the images would dissolve, and my conscious mind would take over?

I squeezed my eyes shut, burying my face in the sleeve of my dressing gown and pictured my bedroom. I was tucked up in bed. Warm, snuggled under the covers.

Yes, that's it.

I had overheated under my duvet, and this nightmare was set to wake me up.

Oh, come on! Just push back the covers and wake up, stand up. Go to the toilet, wander to the bathroom, just move!

Anything to break this damn dream.

I was used to having vivid dreams about this mystery man. They were such a constant in my life that I hardly thought about them anymore. But this was getting ridiculous.

I had my eyes squeezed tightly shut. I dug my nails into the back of the opposite hand and prayed to every deity I could think of.

Nothing happened.

It didn't soften the grasp of the tight claws that circled my chest. It didn't lessen the bite of cold against my face and my hands. Thank goodness I'd remembered to put my dressing gown on before venturing to the door. And bed socks!

SIX

LUCY

The dragon pulled me tighter into his chest as the beating of its wings began to slow, morphing into a glide. I was glad for the gentler movement; the harsh motions were beginning to make me feel sick.

I chanced to open one eye a slit. Just to see what was going on.

We were circling atop the huge castle, over the tallest tower. Below us, people gathered, their heads upturned. From this vantage point they looked the size of ants.

If I could have slapped myself in the face, I would have done so.

The dragon's wing movements slowed almost to a standstill as he lowered us down onto the flagstones of the tower. It was like he'd transported us back in time a thousand years.

I managed to get a better look now and the people looked... human. The men wore formal suits, and the women wore high-necked dresses with fur around the collar. They looked like any wealthy group of people, though prepared for the cold climate.

The dragon set me down, more gently than I was expecting. My socked feet hit the flagstones, and I stumbled, disoriented, as he released his grip on me. He landed just behind me, the shadow of his wings falling across my body before they came to rest.

A man rushed forward with a warm blanket, catching me before I fell, and wrapped me up. He was dressed like a butler from some television drama, right down to the high collar and gloves.

My stress ebbed away slightly. I was impressed with the level of detail and accuracy my subconscious had managed to conjure up for this dream.

"Here you go, miss," he said. "Quickly, come inside. You'll catch your death out here."

I didn't argue as the warmth of the blanket engulfed me, and several hands tugged me forward.

I glanced over my shoulder as I went, just in time to see the dragon transform back into the gorgeous caveman who'd kidnapped me.

He stood in silhouette, and my face flushed as I realized he was naked.

Whoa.

I looked away and tried to focus on getting myself safely inside, but the image of his perfect body was burned into my mind.

I'd never seen a man of that size. His muscles were huge, and his cock was bigger than any I'd seen. How was he real?

I giggled to myself.

He wasn't! I'd dreamed him up, obviously! To be my perfect man. All dark and mysterious, stealing me away to a foreign land. Taking me away from my boring life to a place where he would love me forever and keep me always by his side.

What a joke!

Should I just go with it and see where my imagination took me, or should I try to wake up again?

Not that it had worked the first time. I shook my head; I could think about that once we were in the castle.

The butler opened the door and we stepped inside. The warm air was a welcome change, and I shivered in anticipation of soon being toasty warm.

"Are you all right, miss?" he asked.

"Oh yes, I'm fine." I giggled, hearing the tone of my own voice and distantly admitting I sounded hysterical. "A man who turned into a dragon just kidnapped me from my home. How are you this evening?"

The man cocked his head in such an elegant way that I burst out laughing.

"I'm Lucy, by the way." I stuck out my hand.

I'd been raised to be polite, after all.

The man stared at it, like he wasn't sure what he was supposed to do, before putting his palm against mine.

"I'm James, miss. King Stavrok's head of house."

"Head of house?" I asked with a slight scowl. "You mean, like a manager?"

Sounded just like a butler to me.

James nodded once, then the rest of his words came flowing into my mind.

"Hang on a second, did you just say... king?"

"He did," a man boomed from behind me.

I whirled around to face off with my fantasy kidnapper.

I really hoped this wasn't one of those dreams where I got tied against some wall and ravaged. I had those on occasion, and they embarrassed me for weeks.

"What is going on here? You need to explain, because to me... this is simply..." I searched for the word, my mind exploding in a shower of light as it battled to string a sentence together while he was still so close to me. "This is unacceptable!"

The man laughed. The deep, rich sound rippled over my skin like a lover's caress.

He stalked toward me, his face set with single-minded determination.

"What are you..." I retreated, backing up and away from him until my back pressed flat against a cold stone wall.

He kept coming at me, not slowing his pace in the least.

Part of me was terrified, but as I watched each muscle flex and his intent became clear, my body melted. I knew that look in men; he was going to kiss me.

I moaned when he finally pressed his body against me and cupped my face.

"You're mine," he said with a growl.

His mouth descended, pressing against mine so firmly I gasped. I didn't even get to offer a blistering reply.

If I could have managed one.

He took my lips like they belonged to him. Like they were his territory, ripe for conquering.

My perfect lover.

My brain shut down as years of sexual deprivation soaked up every inch of this man's body against mine.

My hands slid up to his face and my fingers moved through his hair like I needed to touch him just to survive. He rumbled with approval and drew me even closer, his chest pressing against my breasts.

His mouth was magic. As my eyes slid shut, his arms encircled my waist like a vice, and he pressed his thickening cock up against me. A hot jolt of lust shot through me, pooling in my stomach.

I moaned again, shameless, parting my lips and thrusting my tongue into his mouth.

Then he pulled back. Pain sliced through my chest at the loss of him, and I held back a whimper.

"What's wrong?" I whispered.

Would even my fantasy lover reject me? As so many had done before in the real world.

His eyes roamed my face and body with lascivious intent. With an inhuman growl, he grabbed my hand.

"This way," he murmured. His voice was so low I felt it vibrate through my chest.

He led the way along the wide hallway, withdrawing from the crowd of astonished onlookers. I knew I should feel self-conscious after my little display, but I couldn't bring myself to care. This was *my* dream, after all.

Let them look.

I had to run to keep up with his long strides, and I found myself giggling as we hastened along the corridor.

This was an incredible dream! The level of detail was amazing. The stonework, the carved ceiling, the tapestries—even the paintings on the walls. They had a strange otherworldly beauty, like everything here. Their brushwork glowed in the dim, flickering candlelight as we rushed past.

The man, King Stavrok—what kind of a name was that?—pushed open a door, then turned and swung me up into his arms without hesitation.

"Oh, no! I'm too heavy," I squealed, then wanted to slap myself.

This was my fantasy man! As if he couldn't carry my size sixteen butt.

"You're light as a feather." His low tone rippled through my chest as he strode across the floor.

He threw me down onto the massive, four poster bed.

I laughed as I lay back and sprawled over the silk pillows. I was going to be so annoyed when I woke up in my cold bed alone after this. I may as well make the most of it while the dream lasted.

I threw 'playing hard to get' out the window and began

pulling off my dressing gown, eager to get to the good part before the dream ended.

It always pissed me off when I woke up just before the sexy stuff started.

After my dressing gown came my pajamas. I tried to be as seductive as possible, not an easy feat when sprawled out across a huge bed, with a king staring down on me in wonderment.

I giggled again.

"What's funny?" He growled.

"You're a king," I said with the wave of one hand. "Of *course,* you're a king. What else would you be?"

He didn't seem to understand the joke, but he started to undress. Which was what I wanted.

He pushed off the robe he'd put around him, and he was standing before me in all his naked glory.

"Fuck, you're perfect," I sighed as I unbuttoned my pajama top and pushed it away.

The room was warm, with a fire burning and sparking in the grate not far away. I was already flushed as it was, my cheeks burning with anticipation and my stomach tingling.

"As are you," he said.

That sealed the deal for me; this had to be a dream. What real guy would say something like that?

"Ha! Sure, all of this is *so* perfect." I lay back and gestured to my huge thighs, soft tummy, and massive boobs.

He crawled on to the bed, his powerful frame looming over me. He grabbed for my hand and put it against his rock-hard erection.

"Yes."

I gasped as his flesh filled my hand.

"You're exactly the woman for me. You're exquisite."

He slid down and lay on his belly, pushing open my thighs and staring down at my pussy. I covered my face with my hands, feeling the heat rising from my neck, and not in a good way.

Why can't I be cool, even in my own dream?

Oh, fuck it. None of this was real. When would a guy like this ever want a woman like me? What the hell did I have to lose if I threw everything into this night? After all. It was just a dream.

SEVEN

I moved my hands away from my scorching hot cheeks and opened my legs wider, displaying myself to him. He growled with approval and leaned in, licking me with slow, purposeful intent. I whimpered at the sensation, pushing myself up onto my trembling elbows so I could get a better view of him.

Then he licked me again, flicking his heated gaze up to meet mine. The sight was too much, and I collapsed onto the bed, arching my back helplessly, wanting him to come even closer.

He slid his hands firmly beneath my ass cheeks and lifted me up, bringing his food to him.

"Oh, oh God," I said with a moan.

He licked my clit from side to side, then suckled on the tender flesh until I screamed. He did this for an eternity, teasing me, then he brought his mouth to my core and drank from me like he couldn't get enough of my taste on his tongue.

"Oh, please. You've gotta stop." I grabbed for his hair, his shoulders. I was incoherent. I would do anything he asked, anything to make him stop, to come up and cover his body with mine.

My belly coiled tight with want, and my core ached for him. I needed to feel him inside me.

He kissed my inner thighs, his mouth lingering and worshipful, before moving to my belly and giving it equal attention. I slid a hand into his hair, and he crawled further up, sucking on each nipple until I bucked and gasped before he finally arrived back at my mouth.

"I'm going to make you mine," he said.

I nodded. What else could I do?

"Yes. Yes. Please, take me. I need you."

My voice was pitched up and desperate. I'd never begged before in my life.

How undignified.

But that was what dreams were for. Exploring the darkest, most wanton impulses I had. The ones that would never see the light of day.

He lifted my hips and positioned himself so the head of his cock rested against the entrance to my body, and every logical thought flew out of the window.

"Please." I fumbled for something to grab onto, hands curling around his massive biceps. I pulled him closer, offering my mouth for him to kiss me.

And kiss me he did.

He pressed down into my body, his firm chest sliding against my sensitized nipples, and he pushed his tongue into my mouth the moment he thrust his hips forward, impaling me in one smooth stroke.

I broke our kiss to cry out. It had been a long time, and the pressure bordered on painful as my long un-touched tissues stretched to accommodate him.

"You're so tight." He groaned and lay his forehead against mine, not moving.

I wanted to thank him for waiting for me to acclimatize, but I couldn't speak. I couldn't do anything but shudder underneath him, pinned down by his heft and bulk.

My sex throbbed in need. I wrapped my legs around his waist, which took him even deeper inside my body. We groaned in unison, and I looked up into his perfect face, loving the set of his jaw, the flint-like flecks in his ice-blue eyes.

"You're so big," I finally managed to say.

His expression was calm, though a drip of sweat ran down his face, suggesting that he was not as unruffled as he seemed.

I reached up to his face and pulled him down for a kiss, focusing on the mesh of our tongues, the way our mouths caught against each other. The scrape of his stubble against my cheek only heightened my arousal.

He retreated, then thrust home, snapping his hips into mine in a motion that sent the headboard crashing into the wall behind us.

I cried out again, my shout echoing off the stone walls of the bedchamber. The pleasure was too great. He slid a hand up to roll my nipple between his large fingers, and I was done for.

He began to thrust faster and harder and I shuddered as I felt a small climax sweep through my body. He moaned and bit into my shoulder as my pussy rippled around his cock.

I relaxed a little, the release of tension giving my body a moment of reprieve.

Then he began to ride me faster, hitting spots deep inside my body that I'd never known existed. I sank my teeth into the fleshy part of his shoulder and screamed with every thrust of his perfect cock. This was a dream. Who could hear me? I could be as loud as I wanted.

I shoved him, rolling us over, and he allowed me to manoeuvre our bodies until I was above him. If this was a dream, I could be anything I wanted—including a woman who was confident and exciting in bed, impulsive and daring.

Everything I was not in real life.

He landed on his back and pulled me with him, his broad hands settling on my hips, pushing me down onto his cock.

I panted, staring down at his chiseled face and the wild look in his eyes. Slowly, I began to ride him. Up and down on his thick, long cock, rolling my hips and meeting each of his upward thrusts with a downward move of my own.

I threw back my head and closed my eyes, focusing on the feelings of his roughened hands cupping my breasts, catching against my sensitive nipples. His cock thrust up inside me, until I wanted to cry out in ecstasy.

It was happening again. My belly was tightening, the pleasure cresting, sending me over the edge.

I gasped, every sensation in my body building to an incredible crescendo.

And that was when he flipped us over again.

I was on my back, Stavrok pounding into me over and over again. The sounds of our moans and cries echoed through the room until my head was filled with them. It drove me wild knowing such a stoic man was as affected by me as I was by him.

My orgasm began to peak, and I trembled beneath him helplessly as he kept up the force of his thrusts.

"This time, with me." He thrust inside me one more time, and his orgasm pulsed inside me.

It triggered my own release and stars flashed behind my closed eyelids as he filled me with his cum. We shuddered and shook together, grabbing onto one another like a life raft in a storm.

Eventually, he withdrew, and the energy in the room calmed and settled.

I winced at the pain as he pulled out of me, but I couldn't complain as an incredible lethargy stole over my body.

"Oh, my God," I groaned. "This is the best dream ever."

I rolled onto my side and wasn't surprised when he spooned me, his huge body making me feel small. Safe. Loved.

The perfect end to the perfect dream. And tomorrow I would wake up in my safe little world where dragons didn't exist.

Thank goodness.

CHAPTER

EIGHT

LUCY

I rolled onto my back and tried to swim up to the surface of consciousness. It wasn't easy. My mind kept dragging me back down and into the deep sleep I'd been enjoying.

I'd had the craziest, most intense dream of my life last night. Part of me wanted to replay it before I woke up properly. I smirked to myself, eyes still closed.

I had to get up for work.

What time was it? Had I slept through my alarm? It wasn't a weekend, was it?

I reached out and blindly groped around for my phone on the bedside table. The surface my fingers hit was smooth, cold, and unfamiliar and there was no phone to be felt on it.

With a huff, I managed to force my eyes open. I stared up at the ceiling above me. My eyes widened and my stomach sank as my gaze focused, the last vestiges of sleep evaporating.

Was that... a *dragon* carved into my ceiling?

It was.

Holy shit!

I sat bolt upright and whipped my head around, looking left and right.

This isn't my room!

This was the room from the crazy dream I'd had last night.

I looked to the other side of the massive bed and gazed at the indent in the pillow where someone had slept beside me.

My hand flew to my mouth. It couldn't be. No. It wasn't possible. No matter how hard I blinked, the picture didn't change. My eyes weren't deceiving me.

I was in a castle room.

With a wolf skin rug laid over the flagstones and a small fire still simmering in the grate. The bed I was in was huge, with an intricately carved headboard.

Was that an *actual suit of armor* in the corner?

"What the fuck is going on?"

The blankets fell into my lap and my naked breasts tingled in the air. I looked down at myself. My *nude* self. Where the hell had my pajamas gone?

I leaned over the mattress and saw them on the floor, next to the bed—where I'd thrown them last night in my dream.

"Oh...no..."

I brought my arms together, reached my right hand over to my left, and pinched the skin. Hard.

Pain blistered my arm.

"Ow."

I rubbed at the offending limb and bit my lip, moaning. If I wasn't dreaming, then last night was real. And that man I'd had sex with was real. More than that. He was a...

Dragon.

It sounded crazy even in my head, but I could hardly deny the evidence of my own surroundings.

I threw back the covers and jumped out of bed, reaching for my pajamas and pulling them on as fast as I could. My belly was tight and sore. My thighs were still slick with last night's sexual escapades.

Oh, my God.

"How is this possible?"

I pulled at the tie on my dressing gown, tightening it around me. I rushed over to the wall and glanced out the narrow window. It was still snowing. Despite the warmth of the room, I shivered, remembering the wild journey last night.

How the hell am I going to get home?

One of the massive doors opened and I jumped, my heart pounding against my rib cage.

It wasn't the man from last night.

The king, I reminded myself.

A young, rather beautiful woman stepped into the room. Jealousy welled up in me at the sight of her slight figure. Her beautiful face.

"Oh, I'm so sorry, miss. Did I wake you?" she asked as she came forward.

She made a weird move, as though bowing to me in some way. I ignored her. I didn't know what that was all about; I wasn't a queen.

"You didn't. Can you tell me who I should speak to about going home, please?"

I pitched my voice to sound as authoritative as possible, pleased when it didn't tremble.

"Home, miss?" she asked, her eyes big and wide.

"Yes, home." I shook my head, gesturing vaguely at the window, though I didn't know which direction *home* was. "I'm late for work. I have bills to pay. People will be looking for me."

She frowned as if I were speaking a foreign language. I realized how alone I was, in this strange... town? Country?

"If you wouldn't mind... where *am* I right now, exactly?" I twisted my mouth, chagrined. "I had kind of a weird night."

She smiled shyly, but there was something in her eyes that told me she knew exactly what kind of night I'd had. I forced myself to maintain her gaze, praying I wasn't flushed.

"You are in the Kingdom of Bravdok, miss."

"Right..." There was no such place, as far I knew. Then again, I reminded myself, there were no such thing as *dragons* as of yesterday. "And how do I get back to Livia?"

"Livia?"

"Yes, it's a town about an hour outside of Munich." I swallowed. "My home."

"Are you talking about... the human city, miss?"

Now this was just getting *weird*.

"Uh...yes?"

The girl began to back away as though I was scaring *her*, and not the other way around.

What the hell had I fallen into here?

"I think you should speak to the king. He's training downstairs in the armory."

The king? My fantasy lover? The man I'd dreamt about my whole life?

Oh, God. I didn't want to face him after last night. But what choice did I have?

He was obviously the one in charge around here. He was the *king,* after all.

I seemed to have fallen into some crazy medieval wormhole by mistake.

My subconscious told me to pay attention. Though the woman's clothing was ordinary at first glance, there were strange patterns on her sleeves that weren't like anything I'd seen before.

The way she'd said the word *human*, like she wasn't one...

She looked human enough, but her eyes were a shade of amber that gleamed just a little too brightly for my liking.

I pushed down my fear and straightened my spine, brushing

back the hair that had fallen over my face. I wished I could do something about my unkempt appearance.

Whatever. It was time to put on my big girl panties and deal with whatever fate had dealt me here.

"Take me to him, please."

The woman scurried, mouselike, toward the door. Wearing only my dressing gown, I followed her out of the massive suite and into the hallway that looked vaguely familiar.

My gaze skittered over the furnishings, from the magnificent paintings, to the thick rugs that scattered the floor.

This place looked like a fourteenth-century medieval castle. In daylight, I could fully appreciate how gorgeous everything was. Shafts of sunlight pierced the stonework and illuminated the intricate carvings. Dragons were everywhere; in the paintings, roaring from the carvings in the ceiling, even embroidered into the tapestries that covered the high stone walls.

What the hell was I doing in a place like this?

The maid, or servant—whoever my silent companion was— opened a door and indicated the stairs leading down into what I had to assume was a dungeon of sorts.

My belly twisted. First, I'd been kidnapped from my home, and now I was being imprisoned? It just added insult to injury.

"The king is down the stairs, just along the passage," she said. "It comes out to a courtyard. You can't miss it."

I stared, first at the dimly lit stairwell and then back at her. "You expect me to walk down those stairs by myself?"

She nodded. "The king doesn't like to be disturbed when he's training with his fencing master, miss. But, for his mate, I'm sure he will not mind the interruption."

"His *what?*"

Had she just said, 'mate'?

She bobbed another one of those weird curtsies at me and walked away.

I was left standing in an opulent hallway, by myself, staring at the stairwell that may or may not take me to the man who could clear up all this confusion.

At this point, anything could happen.

I waited, hoping that someone would arrive to help me decide whether to venture down, or try and find my own way out of here.

But no one came.

I leaned into the hallway, keeping an eye out for anyone who might push me, and heard the distant sounds of metal clinking against metal.

Had the servant said something about armor?

"Oh, come on." I blew out a breath and shoved my hands into my dressing gown pockets. "You can do this!"

I grabbed hold of the cold stone wall and took a deep breath.

The steps were narrow and crooked, and I took them one at a time, slowly and carefully, focusing on my breathing.

As the ground flattened out, my legs got more and more jelly-like, and I was ready to run and flee at a moment's notice.

No dungeon waited for me at the other end of the narrow corridor. Just a bright, massive courtyard that could have held a tournament, once upon a time.

Inside this courtyard, two bare-chested men fought with broadswords. They grunted with every blow.

I steeled myself against the feelings I knew I would experience when I saw him again. The bastard had kidnapped me. Surely, I'd be furious when I saw him.

But as I stared at him, the only feeling making my belly tighten and my heart pound... was lust. Unfulfilled, deep aching for the man.

God, he was magnificent.

The muscles of his chest and back shone with sweat and bunched with every swing of his sword. The sunlight caught every movement, and his blade cut through the air like an extension of his body. He made every strike look effortless.

When he saw me, he stopped the fight with a simple flick of his hand.

The man next to him let his sword fall and it clattered against the flagstones. His chest heaved with the stress of the fight. He wasn't as big as the king, nor as old, but he was more exhausted from the fight than Stavrok.

My kidnapper turned to address me. "Good morning, my future queen. Did you sleep well?"

The other man bowed to us, falling back to a respectful distance, before practically running away in his haste to get out of there.

Maybe it was the look on my face that caused that? I wasn't sure, but I was glad that he was gone. This first conversation was going to be awkward enough as it was. I'd slept with this man... and I didn't even know him.

I took a couple of careful, measured steps toward Stavrok, tilting my head.

"What did you just call me?" I said, enunciating every word.

I could feel the lust draining away. In its place, there was an icy amount of fury.

Mate? Queen? Had I fallen into the twilight zone?

Stavrok grabbed a towel from the ground and rubbed down his body, tousling his hair as he went. It had the effect of making him even more gorgeously rumpled.

Dammit, concentrate!

"Answer me!"

"Are you always like this first thing in the morning?" He leveled a crooked grin at me, and I flushed, irritated.

I stamped my foot. "No. I am not. When I wake up at home, in my own bed, I'm pretty goddamn happy, actually. But when I wake up in a stranger's bed, in a bloody *castle*... Yeah, I guess I get a little grumpy!"

Ugh! Why do I sound like a petulant child, all of a sudden?

I took some steadying breaths and tried to suppress my anger as he chuckled to himself.

"Can you please just answer the question, King?"

"Please." His gaze was open and friendly in the face of my hostility. "Call me Stavrok."

Tingles coursed over my bare forearms at the sound of his deep voice, and I rubbed my hands over the traitorous skin, fruitlessly attempting to erase the effect he had on me.

"Okay... Stavrok. Can you please explain to me what I'm doing here?"

"What's your name, dear one?"

Heat blushed up my cheeks. He didn't even know my *name*, but he'd made me cum several times the night before.

I'd never had a one-night stand before. Shit, I hadn't even meant to have this one!

"I'm Lucy."

"Ah. Beautiful."

He pulled on a shirt that had been lying next to the towel, hiding his perfect physique from view—which was great for me. My concentration could only improve without the visual distraction.

"I must bathe, and then we shall talk," he said.

He moved to walk past me, and I grabbed for his arm.

"No. Please. Tell me what's going on here. I want to go home."

He turned and slipped his hands around my waist, squeezing me gently against him. "That is not possible, my dear one. We mated last night, and you will stay here and be my queen. The fates have already decided."

Despite the calm and happy feelings his touch brought me, his words shattered me.

I broke away from him.

"*What?* No! You can't do that! You kidnapped me last night, and now I want to go home!"

Said every kidnap victim, ever.

He smiled softly. "I'm sorry, but that's not possible, especially as you may be carrying the heirs to my kingdom."

"Heir*s*?" I squealed.

How many did he expect me to conceive after only one night?

"Yes. Dragons shifters are known to have up to four babes at a time, but as you are human, it may be different with us."

"Dragon shifters... Four babies... Oh, my God, I have to sit down."

My mind was whirling, the blackness beginning to cloud my mind.

I was going to faint for the first time in my life.

And then I did, and the whole world, such as it was, went black.

NINE

STAVROK

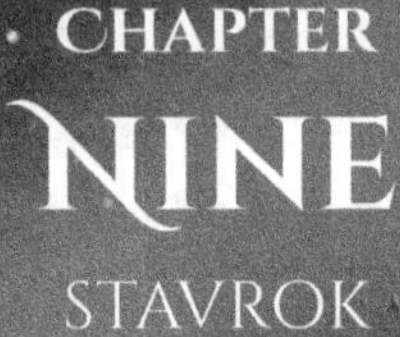

I rushed forward and caught my mate before she hit the ground.

"Humans..." I muttered, shaking my head as I swept her limp form up into my arms.

I didn't know if this swooning phase was normal for Lucy, or an early sign of her pregnancy. Either way, I needed to call my physician to attend to her.

I took the stairs two at a time, cradling her in my arms, and shouted for assistance. My voice carried down the corridor, and a couple of maidservants came running at once.

"Lucy has fainted." I hefted her up, my stance protective. I forced myself not to scowl. "I'm going to take her back to my bedroom. Can you get the physician here as soon as possible?"

"Yes, sire."

They bobbed a curtsey in unison and scurried off.

I strolled to my bedroom slowly, loving the feel of my mate in my arms.

Last night had not been what I'd expected. I'd thought I would go to my mate and talk to her, perhaps even get to know her.

Instead, my shifter had recognised its mate and the dragon had ripped through me so fast, I had no control over him.

Then he'd taken her.

Kidnapped her.

It was something I had sworn I would never do to any woman. But I had. Just as my father had done before me, and my grandfather before him. This woman was my undoing, the thorn in my side. She'd broken through my defences, my carefully built control.

I entered our bedroom and laid her down on the bed.

Lucy had been incredible last night. Her passion and intensity had perfectly matched my own. She was utterly gorgeous, an ideal fit in every way.

I'd been pleasantly surprised that my mate would be my match in the bedroom. She'd taken my body as though she had a right to it. Which, of course, she did.

Now she was acting like she didn't even know who I was, or what had gone on last night.

Was that normal for humans?

The door opened, and the royal physician walked in, bowing when he saw me lingering at the foot of the bed.

"Hello, Arnold," I said. "I'm sorry to disturb you so early in the day. My mate fainted, and I am unsure if that is normal for her kind."

"Your mate, sire?" The physician's eyebrows shot upwards. "I didn't know that you'd found your intended queen."

I indicated the woman on the bed and didn't answer him past that. I couldn't blame him for his shock. I was still struggling with the idea myself.

Only yesterday, I'd been completely alone. A bachelor king, burning with frustration at the lack of change and transition with my life. No queen. No heirs. Nothing to give me the happiness that I saw in those who governed my neighboring kingdoms.

Overnight, everything had changed. My dragon had found its mate. I'd found my queen. And she may be pregnant already.

The physician checked her over gently before eventually turning to me. "It seems as though she has simply fainted, sire. When she wakes up, we can do some tests if you wish it."

"Thank you. I shall call you if we deem that necessary."

He bowed again and moved away from the bed as Lucy began to stir.

I couldn't help myself from reaching out. I walked around the side of the bed and touched her forehead, checking for a fever as her eyelids fluttered open.

There was a recognition of sorts, and for a split second her eyes softened. Then a blazing anger raced across her green irises, twisting up her face with a rage that came over her like a sudden storm.

"You!" she cried as she sat up, then grimaced before slumping back against the headboard.

"Don't move so fast, my love," I said. "You fainted. You must rest."

She swallowed strangely. I picked up the jug from the bedside table and poured her a glass of water. Thank goodness for servants.

"Here," I said, offering her the glass. "Sip this slowly and try to stay calm. No one is going to hurt you here, I promise."

She took the glass, though she eyed it as though I may have put poison in it.

After a moment's hesitation, she took a sip, then pressed a trembling hand to the side of her face and glared at me. She still looked pale, though color was slowly returning to her cheeks.

"Are you well? Should I call the physician back?"

It began to dawn on me then how little I knew about humans in general. Was their physiology exactly as ours was? Should I be worried about our offspring's health?

"No. I'll be fine, I think." Sighing, she set down the glass on the bedside table again, then pulled her knees up to her chest and wrapped her arms around them.

I sat down on the edge of the bed and tightened my fingers into the blankets around me. I ached to touch her, to roll her beneath me. To sink into her body once again and taste the essence of her lips.

But she was as frosty as the snow-topped cliff faces beyond the window.

"Stavrok... what am I doing here?"

Such a simple question; such a complicated answer. I stood up and moved around, pacing like a caged lion.

May as well tell her the truth.

"You're here because a sorceress told me you were my destiny, and that I ought to seek you out."

Lucy's eyes opened wide, then she nodded slowly. "Okay... assuming I believe you, what, pray tell, were you planning on doing with me once you found me? Because I hope the whole kidnapping thing was an oversight on your part."

She fiddled with the edge of the bedspread, glaring at the snowscape outside.

I frowned. Where was the confident, sensual woman from the night before?

"Lucy, I don't understand why you are so shocked about everything this morning. As I recall it, last night you had no objections to sharing my bed."

Redness blossomed over her cheeks as she glared at me. "Last night, I thought you were a *dream!* How could I have known, honestly, that you weren't? You turned into a dragon, for fuck's sake!"

She whipped her hair over her shoulder, and I got the strong impression that she still wasn't fully convinced any of this was real.

My eyebrows rose at her language. It wasn't exactly fitting for a queen, but who was I to judge at this point of our relationship?

She wasn't wrong, was she? I *had* taken her.

I shifted, uncomfortable now. "I suppose, for a human, dragons are uncommon creatures. But here, everyone can do it."

"Everyone? Even the children?" Lucy asked, her mouth dropping open.

"No, not the children." It was strange to have to relay such common knowledge to someone. Like I was describing the color of the sky to someone who was blind. "We begin shifting when we hit maturity. Around thirteen, fourteen, depending on the person."

"Okay, but you still haven't answered the question of why you grabbed me, or why everyone keeps bowing to me, or why on *earth* you said that thing before about me conceiving your babies. How many babies are we talking about? And why would you even assume I'd be *pregnant* after one night?"

The questions were coming hot and fast, and a laugh bubbled up and out of me before I could suppress it.

"Which would you like me to answer first?"

She crossed her arms over her chest.

"Stavrok."

A wave of something I'd never experienced passed over my back, before creeping up and over my face. A cold, yet totally invigorating sensation that made my dragon shiver all over.

I approached the bed and reached for Lucy, intent on sharing the sensation with her.

She jumped away from me so fast I barely saw her until she was over by the fireplace.

"No! We are *not* getting into bed together again until I know what's going on!"

I couldn't help but grin. She certainly wasn't ruling it out, which of course I didn't expect her to.

Even *this* angry, it was reassuring to know that she wasn't making any declarations that she knew she couldn't keep.

I smiled at her. "Let's make a deal. You'll let me escort you to breakfast, my dear one, and I'll tell you all you wish to know about how you came to be here."

She seemed to need a lot of information so she could process everything herself, an unusual characteristic in a female of my kind.

They were much more submissive, which was probably why I found them no challenge.

Lucy, on the other hand, would keep life interesting.

"I guess I could eat," she grumbled, but I could tell she was calming down.

It suddenly occurred to me that she was wearing the bedclothes she'd arrived here in and didn't have anything else.

As delicious as it would be to eat breakfast with her naked, I got the sense that suggestion wouldn't be welcome right now. She looked ready to get up and go home, back to the human world, and I couldn't let her leave.

Not now. Not ever.

TEN

STAVROK

I pulled on the servants' bell that dangled from the roof by my bed and within moments, James stepped through the door.

"Yes, sire?"

"We're ready for breakfast." I turned toward Lucy. "Would you prefer to eat here or in the dining room?"

"The dining room," she answered quickly. Too quickly.

I quirked an eyebrow at her, then turned to James.

"Could you bring some things for Lucy to wear today? And we require the royal seamstresses to take her measurements. She'll need a full wardrobe."

"I won't be staying that long," Lucy interjected.

I ignored her comment and waited for James to leave before turning back to her. "I need a shower. Would you like to join me?"

She shook her head and I smiled.

The blush to her full cheeks said otherwise, but I was happy to allow her the illusion of control and space while she became comfortable with me again.

That didn't mean I couldn't tease her a little.

I stripped off my sweat-soaked shirt and threw it to the floor. Next, I unbuttoned the fly and pushed them past my hips, letting them gather around my ankles. I glanced at the bed but Lucy was turned away, focused intently on the scenery out the window.

I grinned to myself.

I worked hard every day to keep my body strong, fit, and ready for a war that could come at any moment. But I wasn't oblivious to the fact that womenfolk enjoyed my bulk and musculature.

I wanted my mate to desire me in the same way. I certainly wanted her.

I turned and sauntered toward the shower, feeling the heat of her gaze on my back. I glanced over my shoulder and caught her looking just as she whirled away.

I flipped on the shower head and stood beneath the warm water, letting the heat sink into my tired muscles.

I'd found my mate! She was here. The idea was finally resonating with me on a deeper level. All those years of emptiness would be behind me. The only thing that remained was for Lucy to accept my world, and all the changes that her new life would bring.

I'd never thought my queen would be human, or that she wouldn't know our ways. The concept of shifting was completely foreign to her, coming as she did from a world without magic.

The memory of grabbing her the night before now felt surreal, strangely out of body. Usually, I remained lucid when the dragon emerged, but this had been different. My shifter had taken over completely in a way that it never had before, and I'd been dragged along for the ride.

Perhaps that was what had happened to my ancestors also?

I'd always thought the way my father and grandfather had grabbed their brides had been primitive and barbaric, but the drive from our shifter to claim our fated mate was far stronger than I had anticipated.

Never mind that now. I've found her, at last!

Well, it had been Queen Marienne who had found her for me. She had sensed her through the magical boundary and handed me the key to a puzzle I'd been trying to solve my whole life. At the thought, a cold feeling washed over my skin. There was something about King Magnik that I didn't wholly trust, and I wasn't sure what role Marienne played in that scenario. There seemed to be no love lost between the king and his queen, but could that be a ruse, to lull me into complacence?

I couldn't guarantee that Marienne hadn't taken something from inside my head after she put Lucy into it. Nor could I understand why she'd want to help me in such a way and not demand payment.

The uncertainty weighed on me. I knew that, if it came to a choice between the payment or the woman, I was keeping Lucy no matter what. I could already feel our connection strengthening with each passing moment. My need was growing, to keep her safe, healthy, and satisfied.

Our bond would only grow with time and age. My own parents were besotted with each other until the day they died.

People were talking in the other room and I switched off the shower, interested to see what my servants had brought Lucy and what they were saying.

I toweled dry my body and grabbed a pair of comfortable pants from a nearby shelf.

The high voices of the women overlapped one other, chattering and gossiping away nineteen to the dozen. Lucy laughed at something one of them said, and my lips twitched up into a smile.

She was my mate, which meant fate had chosen her to be my queen, to rule my people. I wanted her to belong here, to feel this was her home.

I walked out of the bathroom to see Lucy standing in a simple shift dress, her luscious breasts pressed high and together, creating a cleavage that called to me to press my face against.

"Sire, how may dresses were you wanting for your new mate?" The seamstress asked me.

Lucy's gaze flicked straight to me. "What is this *mate* business? I don't understand it at all."

She was holding her arms out and turning this way and that as the seamstress asked, her earlier protests at odds with her actions.

"Get something on and we'll talk over breakfast," I assured her, before turning to the woman on the floor with pins stuck in her mouth. "As many as she will require. I trust she will let you know once she's had a chance to settle in."

I flicked my hand and the woman got up and curtsied deeply. "Yes, Your Highness."

She grabbed her materials and left the room.

Lucy drew up the dress and stockings they'd left for her in the meantime, draped over the back of a chair. The dress was finely woven, with rich purple hue. Befitting for a queen.

"I'm not really a dressy girl." She held up the dress, turning this way and that in front of my tall mirror that stood against the wall opposite the bed head. "I'm more of a jeans and t-shirt sort of woman."

"Why is that?" I asked her as I pulled on a shirt and my shoes.

"It's just easier to hide... all of this," she said, gesturing to her shapely, perfect body.

I laughed. "Why should you hide anything? Your body is strong, dear one. Healthy, beautiful. You should carry yourself with pride."

Lucy looked down at the ground and I reached over and touched her chin, tipping her head up and staring down into her eyes.

"In my eyes, you are perfection itself." I leaned closer, dropping my voice to a whisper. "Believe me, if I had my way, I'd strip both of us to nothing at all and devour you all over again this instant."

A smile trembled on her lips. "Do you like bigger women? Is that it? Because I can tell you, where I come from, men like you don't want women like me."

"Women like you?"

Confusion filled me. What did she mean?

"Yeah. Frumpy, chubby, big girls."

I let my hands run down her body, pausing at her tiny waist and then gripping her ass. She yelped in surprise but didn't fight me.

"Lucy, I don't 'like' big girls—I like you. *All* of you. I'm not sure how stupid human men are, but anyone who made you feel less than you are, is an imbecile. You're perfect in every way, and I desire you more than any other woman I've ever met. Can't you feel how much I want you?"

I pressed her pelvis closer to mine, where I was sure she could feel the hardening of my cock in my pants.

She bit her lip in an innocent, vulnerable way and then whispered, "Thank you."

It was too much for me—I had to kiss her.

I dropped my head and she lifted hers up to meet mine. Our lips met and a mutual moan was pulled from both our mouths.

Oh, God.

I wrapped my arms around her and pulled her closer, sliding my tongue into her mouth and tasting her. She gripped my face with her hands and held me to her, and I let the kiss go on and on.

My cock throbbed and my lust swirled in my heated blood, but I knew that the next time I took my mate to bed, it needed to be something she was desperate for.

I'd never taken a woman against her will, and I never would.

Finally, I pulled back and stared down at her beautiful face.

Her cheeks were rosy, her green eyes dazed. Her lips were blood red from my kisses.

"Shall we go to breakfast?" I asked her and I could see her disappointment and rushed to reassure her. "I'd love to take you back to bed, so if you'd rather stay and make love first..."

She stepped away. "No, you're right. Breakfast. Talking. I'm sorry, but your kisses are just..."

"Intoxicating?" I finished for her.

She frowned. "Is that how everyone else feels about them, too?"

I laughed. "Who's everyone else? The women of my past were not interested in my kisses. I was referring to your taste for me. If my kisses have half the effect on you that your kisses have on me, I'm surprised we're still standing here dressed."

She giggled and tightened the belt around her waist. "Well, we have to be a little bit smart about this."

I took her hand and pulled her to the door and into the corridor, leading the way to the dining hall. Though I didn't say it, I was looking forward to eating in company for once. It was depressing, eating alone in a room designed to seat twenty.

I shook the thought away and turned to her. "Do you always do what is right, what is logical?"

That was a great attribute for a queen, though I hoped when it came to the bedroom, she would be more adventurous than that.

"Yes, I try to. But... I do have a bit of a temper, and I can sometimes be..."

"Less than perfect? Yes, I know that feeling well."

She smiled at me with an understanding that we hadn't shared yet and there was a moment that I recognized, of our souls linking and connecting.

It stole my breath away.

My God, what would I do if she left me now?

I shook away the feelings of dread and loneliness that such a thought gave me.

"Here we go." I pushed open the door and led her inside to the massive dining table. The chef and maidservants stood by the table, welcoming us with smiles.

As I had ordered, it was laden with everything anyone could possibly want for breakfast. Fresh breads piled high, a selection of jams and butter to accompany them, hot eggs and sausages on silver trays, and fruit and berries of all kinds. Jugs of sweet wine complemented the spread.

I nodded, satisfied.

I wanted Lucy to know that I could provide for her. She would want for nothing while she was here.

I looked over at my chef who still hovered nearby. "You've outdone yourself."

She smiled, then tapped the side of her nose. "I heard it was an important day, sire."

I walked to the head of the table and held out a chair for my mate.

"Thank you, Cherie." I smiled, waving her off. "That will be all for now."

I had a big job ahead of me. I had to convince my mate to stay with me. Even though I considered myself a civilized man, I didn't want to see what would happen if she tried to leave me.

My dragon wouldn't like that.

ELEVEN

STAVROK

My chef smiled as she left, accompanied by the maidservants, and I focused back on Lucy.

"Let's sit."

We took our places at the huge dining table and I glanced over at my mate.

"Wow, this looks amazing." Lucy smiled as big and excited as a child with new toys.

She obviously liked to eat and enjoyed food as I did, but something told me not to mention it.

I gestured toward the table. "Please, dig in. Take as much as you want."

I reached for the hot bread rolls and smothered them with butter, before grabbing the meat.

Lucy took a few berries and eyed the bread on my plate with envy.

"Please, eat." I pushed two rolls onto her plate and she practically shoved them straight off again.

"It's good food, I promise." I shot her a crooked smile. "Not poisoned."

She gave me a reluctant smile, before she sighed, fiddling with her fork. "It's not that... I can't. It's the carbs..."

She trailed off, looking longingly at the plates piled with steaming morsels.

I laughed. There were no such stupid rules in my kingdom. "Lucy, you're in a kingdom that must seem magical to you, a world full of dragons and castles. You've accepted these, yes? Why deny yourself the pleasure of good food?"

Her face twisted strangely before it cleared. She nodded, like she finally saw my logic.

"God, you're right. To hell with my diet!" She wrinkled her nose in a manner I found adorable. "They never work anyway."

She tore into the bread, slid a sausage into a roll, and bit into it in a way that had me groaning with need.

"You okay?" she asked, and I took a long drink of the sweet wine they'd poured for us.

"Yes."

She gestured with her hands that I should go on, but I didn't know where to start. I didn't know how to convey how much I wanted her. The best I could do, for now, was deflect.

"You have questions. What is it you want to know?"

She swallowed and glared at me, but this time there was a note of playfulness in her expression that made my chest spark with hope.

"Tell me why I'm here, for one thing," she said.

I leveled my gaze at her, considering. "It may be easier if I go back a bit and explain a few things. Is that all right?"

She nodded, sipping at the water in front of her. "Sure, tell me everything."

Where to begin?

"I may as well tell you about my history. My parents were married for thirty years before they both died a few winters ago."

Her face was stricken, pale and pained. "Oh, I'm so sorry."

"They died together," I said shortly. One day, I would tell her the full truth. But the story was a long one, and I didn't want it to cast a pall over our happiness. "It was what they would have wanted."

A soft smile filtered across Lucy's face. "Yeah, I think I can understand that. I've dreamt about that sort of love, but never experienced it."

And neither have I... until now.

"Well, you see, most dragon shifters have a mate that the fates choose for them. When we find them, we know them by their smell. There's an instant attraction. They are our perfect match in every way..." I dropped my gaze. "My parents had that. In fact, my father kidnapped my mother right out of her village and never took her home again."

Lucy laughed. "God, that must run in your family."

I grinned at her. "It does. My grandfather was the same. When our dragons see their fated mate, there is no holding him back. It is—it was, last night—uncontrollable."

"Hang on a second. Are you telling me that you think I'm your... fated mate, or whatever it's called?" She stared at me like I was insane.

"I don't just think it," I said, my voice solemn. "I know it. The feelings I'm experiencing, the way I shifted with no control last night, my dragon recognized its mate. I've been waiting for you for... a long time."

I didn't want to say something corny like 'forever' or 'my whole life' but now that I had her, I knew what it felt like to have that hole in my heart filled.

I wasn't letting her go.

"But that's impossible! I'm not like you!" she spluttered. "I'm human, in case you haven't noticed."

"Yes, I know. I don't know what sort of offspring you will

have, but Fate has chosen you for me, and Fate is never wrong." I smiled. "I have every faith in you, Lucy."

I didn't want to tell her that Marienne believed she had a dragon shifter ancestor somewhere down the line. That may be too much for the woman to take in right now, on top of everything else.

Her face creased up, and I longed to pull her close and soothe her.

"But, but, but—no! Stavrok, come *on*. You can't be serious about this. Fated mates... soul mates... it's not real. I don't know *what* you felt last night, or why we..." Her cheeks flushed. "But it isn't because some mythical thing like fate made us do it!"

I just grinned at her. She hadn't fled the room screaming yet. There was hope for this strong little human.

"What did you feel last night, Lucy? Tell me."

Her confident gaze dropped away from me.

I leaned forward. "Because for me, it wasn't a choice. I *had* to have you. You were the most beautiful woman I'd ever seen in my life, and I felt like I would die if I didn't kiss you."

Her eyes came up and met mine, and the fragility in her eyes broke my heart.

I reached out and took her hand, cradling it between my palms.

"I know you must be feeling lost and extremely overwhelmed at this point in time," I said, "but I need you stay with me, at least until we know if you're pregnant or not."

She stared down at her plate. Her eyes were filled with tears, but when she spoke her voice was strong. "Why? You must know that I can't simply vanish off the face of the planet. I have a job. I have friends! They'll all come looking for me soon enough."

I admired her courage. Even lost and disoriented as she was, she held her ground.

"We have access to the internet in some parts of the castle.

Perhaps you could email them and tell them you've jumped on a plane for an unexpected holiday? Two weeks, that's all I'm asking for, Lucy. Can't you see that this is an opportunity to fulfill all of your wildest dreams?"

No woman had ever reacted like this to finding their soulmate —let alone finding out that their soulmate was a *king*. She would want for nothing for the rest of her life, and yet she was acting like I had given her a prison sentence.

"But my job. What if they fire me?"

I waved my hand around the room. "Then I will fill your bank account with whatever money you need. That is of no consequence to me. You are my first priority, now."

"Oh... I..."

I could tell she had nothing to say, and the topic of money seemed to embarrass her, which was interesting.

"If you need money..." I began.

Her gaze snapped to mine, and her tone was flinty. "I don't need money, thank you. I've paid off most of my house, completely by myself."

I tilted my head and gave her a broad smile. I had no idea what that meant. I was born into a royal family and would never have to pay for any piece of real estate for as long as I lived.

"You'll stay, then?" I pressed.

"You said..." Her voice was small, careful. "If I'm not pregnant, I can go home?"

No!

As much as my dragon resisted the idea of her leaving, she also hadn't asked what would happen if she *was* pregnant, and therefore I didn't need to tell her I would be using every opportunity to ensure it.

"Well..." I said, trying to balance the truth with a comfortable white lie.

Luckily, I didn't need to think of one, because she kept talking.

"The odds that I'm pregnant are low." She tilted her head, counting the days off on her fingers. "I'm quite late in my cycle, and at my age... we only slept together once. It's not likely, is all."

I grinned at her. She clearly had no idea how strong the bond between us was. If there was any chance at all of her becoming pregnant, then she already would be.

"How old are you, Lucy?"

"Thirty-three. And you?"

"Forty-two."

She gaped at me. "You don't look anywhere near that."

I shrugged. "Our shifter genes keep us young. So, my beautiful mate, the woman who will be my queen if you decide to stay in this land of Fire and Ice, do we have a deal?"

I stuck out my hand and she looked at my fingers like they might bite her.

"You know that saying things like that to me, a perfect stranger, makes you sound totally insane, right?" she asked.

"I wouldn't say we're strangers, Lucy. Not after last night... would you?"

She shook her head slowly. "I guess not..."

I kept my hand out, wanting her reassurance that she wouldn't run away the first chance she got. Not that an unaccompanied human would get far in this climate, but she was far too precious to lose to our brutal weather.

"Two weeks, you say?" She pursed her full lips. "And I get to use your computer?"

I nodded. She could do whatever she wanted, if it was within the castle walls.

"Absolutely," I said. "I want you to meet everyone in the castle. Then I'll take you out and show you our town."

She put her hand into mine, and a current of awareness passed over my skin, making a growl rise in the back of my throat.

"All right then. You have a deal," she said.

TWELVE

The excitement fluttering through my belly was unlike anything I'd ever felt.

It was like waiting for an exam, a first date, and the beginning of a roller coaster all at once.

Stavrok spent the morning showing me his favorite parts of the castle. It was truly beautiful, like stepping into a fairy tale. He showed me his parents' portrait in the entrance hall, and the family tapestry hanging beside it. He drew me close and whispered that my name would be embroidered there before long, the glittering golden threads entwined with his, and I fervently hoped he couldn't hear my pulse fluttering at the thought.

We headed out, hand in hand, into the brisk morning air. I was glad for the thick scarf and muff a maid had brought me, because the weather was far chillier than I was used to.

Stavrok walked me down the narrow, cobblestoned path into the little town that lay below the castle. He took pleasure in introducing me to passers-by as we went, and it charmed me that he seemed to know so many of his subjects on sight and had a vested interest in their activities.

The town itself was a strange combination of modernity and old-world charm. The technology seemed to be similar to ours, but there were open-air markets that could've been pulled straight from another age, and I spotted apothecaries selling herbs and crystals that I'd never seen before.

The people were red-cheeked and happy, the streets were clean and inviting, and the castle loomed over everything with a majestic beauty.

As we wandered back toward the castle, I gestured to the people around me.

"You said that you were self-sustainable. How do you manage that in such cold weather?"

The chill in the air had me pulling the cloak around me even tighter.

I didn't know how it was possible, to go from my home, where we were enjoying a mild spring, to this place, where there was snow on the ground and the tip of my nose was frozen.

"We eat seasonally," Stavrok said. "Being dragon shifters, our diet does contain a high meat component. We only grow hardy animals that survive our winters."

"What are your winters like if *this* is spring?"

Stavrok laughed. "It gets colder, certainly. All homes in town have fireplaces and a great heating system."

"And if someone can't afford to pay their bills?"

"Their bills?" He quirked his eyebrow at me as though he didn't know what I meant.

"Yes, for electricity, water. How does everyone pay for that?"

He grinned. "The royal family pays for the entire town, in all ways. As long as the townspeople are doing their jobs, all the essential amenities are taken care of."

I gaped at him, shivering as he opened one of the castle's great oak doors. I ducked inside, the heat enveloping me like a hug.

"So, there's no money?"

"Of course, there's money. We use a similar currency to the Euro, but when it comes to the basics of life—things like water, sewerage, heating, even food if the family is struggling due to illness—the castle takes care of it."

I stared at him, shocked to the core that there was such a place. "I wish our government did the same thing. There are so many homeless, struggling people..."

I shook my head, trying not to think about the depressing parts of the human world.

So many starving...

"Would you like some lunch?" he asked.

I looked around. Surely there were things he needed to attend to?

"I'm all right for the moment, although a shower and then access to a computer would be great," I said. "I really need to write to my work to let them know what's going on."

Or a version of it, anyway.

I'd meant to find the computer straight after breakfast, but Stavrok had wrapped me up in a cloak and encouraged me to come out with him and meet his people.

And how could I say no to a tour of his beautiful lands?

I smiled up at Stavrok. "Thank you so much for the tour. I loved it. Especially the shop full of all those silks. The clothes were spectacular."

Some of the fashions were far too feminine for me, or more feminine than I'd ever allowed myself to be. My job demanded simple and comfortable clothes. All that lace, silk, and ruffles, those intricate buttons—they weren't designed to end up covered in poster paint.

Modern women in my town were either high-powered career women or stay at home moms. I didn't really fit comfortably into either group.

"The dressmaker will return this evening," he said. "You can order anything you like from that shop. They'll have it made up for you to your specifications."

"But…" I wavered. "I won't be staying that long, surely?"

Besides, how would I pay for any of it? I didn't have any money on me.

Stavrok reached out for my hands and pulled me closer. His burning gaze made my knees weaken, and I moaned softly.

"Shall I join you in the shower?"

Images swirled in my head, of steam, and heat, and cold tiles at my back.

I'd always had a fantasy of having hot shower sex up against a wall, but no man had ever come close to fulfilling it for me.

How could they when I weighed more than most of my ex-boyfriends?

With Stavrok, I could see him easily overcoming my weight and clumsiness.

But the last thing I wanted to do was make him think that I had decided to stay, or that we were developing a relationship I wasn't certain about yet.

"I'd rather stay clean after my shower, thank you very much."

Stavrok kissed me, his lips tasting like snow, and sin.

I pushed away from him, the heat of his chest soaking into my palms as I tried to put some much-needed space between us.

"And I'm pretty sure, King Stavrok, that you have more important things to do than show me around and have showers in the middle of the day."

Stavrok grinned. "I do have a kingdom to run, it's true, but I'd prefer to have a shower with you, more than anything else."

When we were a respectable distance from each other, I could finally breathe more easily. "Please, let me do what I need to do, then I'll be more comfortable."

"More comfortable?" he asked, tilting his head.

"Yes, I have obligations that I need to fulfill. My work, my parents..."

I could hardly believe that I'd just left my whole world behind.

Then again, the day-care center probably assumed I was in bed sick, and my parents only called weekly.

That wasn't what rattled me, though. What disturbed me most was how little I'd thought about it all morning. I'd allowed myself to get swept up in Stavrok's icy world, seduced by more than the man himself.

This place called out to me like a siren song. Even though it had only been one night, it was the other world that was starting to feel like the dream.

Stavrok took my hand and held it as walked through the castle. "Well, after you finish all of that, I will meet you for dinner. I think you may like my proposal."

I wasn't sure I liked the sound of that. "What sort of proposal?"

The wolflike grin that sparked Stavrok's teeth made me jump.

"Wait and see. Until then, you need a guide. I'll have one sent to your room."

"What do you mean, a guide? Like your chief of staff?"

Stavrok backed away from me. He must have finally realized that he did indeed have things to do. "Not exactly. James runs everyone and everything, so he'll be somewhere making sure the house isn't burning down without me at the helm. But I'll send someone you'll like, I promise."

He waved, and strode off, the sounds of his leather heels tapping along the hallway until he disappeared into a room.

I sighed and let the happiness that I'd been holding at bay filter into my mind and fill me up.

What am I doing? This is utterly crazy.

I should be working out a way home, plotting my escape, but instead I was luxuriating in all this enjoyment.

Worst of all, memories of the heated moments from last night kept cropping up in my mind at the most inopportune times.

I wandered back to our room–*Stavrok's* room—and soon found myself alone in the large, hot shower.

The bathroom was fitted out with every modern convenience. The towel racks were heated, as were the flagstones underfoot. The walk-in shower had a giant overhead waterfall built into the wall, and there was a huge bathtub, sunken into the floor, with jets embedded in the sides.

And yet this was a castle.

If I didn't feel so awake, I could probably convince myself that I was still dreaming, because not much was making sense at this point.

It took a while before I could properly feel my toes again, but when I did, I was glad of it. It was cold here, much colder than I was used to. These dragon shifters were obviously immune to it, but I was not.

Maybe they ran hotter than I did? I swallowed, thinking of Stavrok's chest pressed up against mine. Even through my clothes, he was a total furnace. I would have to take precautions next time I went outside. Thicker socks, more layers. Maybe I could find some earmuffs. I giggled at the thought.

Tilting back my head, I let the warmth of the water flow over me.

What am I doing?

Rearranging my life around Stavrok? I'd only known the guy for one night, and all his promises seemed way too good to be true.

Fairy tales like this didn't happen to women like me. I should get out of here before I got too attached. I didn't want to get myself hurt.

But what was I really rushing back to?

A job that paid me just above minimum wage to help raise other peoples' children, because I didn't have any of my own?

"Hello! Lucy! Can I come in?"

The sound of a young, chirpy female voice echoed through the room.

Did she want to come *into* the bathroom? I wasn't sure how comfortable I was with that.

"Just give me a second," I called. "I'll be out in a moment."

I switched off the water and grabbed a fluffy towel from a nearby rack. I rubbed the towel over every part of me. The room was so warm I was comfortable, but the knowledge of a stranger in the adjacent room made me want to get dressed as soon as possible.

Since my clothes were in the other room, I ventured out into the bedchamber wearing only the bath towel.

A young woman, who reminded me of our day-care center receptionist, greeted me with a beaming smile.

Her curly brown hair tumbled over her slight shoulders, and her eyes were the brightest blue I'd ever seen on a person.

Then again, those striking eyes seem to be common around these parts.

"Hello," I said, holding the towel tight against my huge breasts, which as usual threatened to spill out over the top.

"Hey! I'm Cass, His Majesty's cousin," the woman said. "And you must be the famous Lucy. It's so great to meet you!"

Cousin… All right. I could deal with that.

THIRTEEN

I lifted my chin and answered, "Yes, I am."

Cass clapped her hands together like an excited child. "This is going to be brilliant! When Stavrok told me you'd arrived, I couldn't believe it. People have been waiting for my cousin to marry for like... ages. Years! And now he's finally got his mate!"

I groaned and rolled my eyes. "Why does everyone keep jumping forward, planning out my whole life for me? I met Stavrok last night—last *night!* I'm not about to just marry him tomorrow because he thinks I'm some mythical mate... thing..."

The girl's face balked, her smile turning upside down as she went pale. "Oh...."

I clenched my teeth and forced some deep breaths.

"Look, Cass. You seem lovely, and I would really enjoy a rundown of how things work around here if you can spare the time, but I'm human. And I'm not used to being told what I must and mustn't do, so if you don't mind..."

She giggled. "You sound just like Stavrok."

That stopped me in my tracks. "In what way?"

"He's always said he wouldn't marry just because it was expected, and that he wouldn't succumb to the fated mates curse like his father did. But look at you! He snatched you out of a human town, didn't he?"

"Um..." I bit my lip. "Yes."

"I knew it!" She began pulling clothes from a huge oak wardrobe on the other side of the room. "The servants have left some things in here for you. Here. Try some stuff on. I wanna see!"

Cass wasn't looking in my direction, but I was still self-conscious. I didn't have much of a choice about changing in front of her, and as a fully grown woman, I knew I should get over myself. She was a girl. I was a girl.

Before I chickened out, I dropped the towel to the ground and grabbed for the thick stockings and the long-sleeved shift that had been laid out on the bed for me.

Layers, that was what I needed. Layers.

Over the shift, I slid on a soft, fine-knit sweater, following it with a low-necked garment that seemed to be a cross between a sweater and a dress. I smoothed it down against my body, finally feeling like I would be warm enough to face the rest of the day.

I didn't want to venture outside again, though. I'd always imagined huge castles of this kind to be drafty and uncomfortable, but with the crackling fire in the grate, I felt cosy as hell.

"That's better." I shuddered, remembering the icy air outside. "Goodness, it's cold here."

Cass turned around with her big smile. "You'll get used to it soon enough."

I gave her a smile in return, although my stomach twinged with unease.

That was my worry. I was already *far* too used to this place. I kept letting my guard down without realizing, sliding into the role Stavrok seemed so eager for me to play.

Cass was looking at me expectantly, and I shook my head to clear it.

Did she say something?

"Wow, you're miles away," she said, her eyes merry. "I said, you look the part! You should ask Stavrok about jewelry. I know he has some of his mother's old pieces squirreled away. You'll be the belle of the ball when the other royals come to dine here."

"What do you mean?" I asked, but Cass was too busy rummaging through the contents of the wardrobe.

As king, it was clear Stavrok had duties to his kingdom and people. I wondered what my duties would be, if I stayed here.

Hostess? Peacemaker? Diplomat?

I swallowed. I wasn't qualified for this— I couldn't even keep the peace through Christmas dinner with my extended family, let alone organize a feast for such important guests!

"You okay? You look like you've seen a ghost." Cass put her hand on my arm, frowning, and I jumped at the contact.

"Yeah," I managed to say, giving her a shaky smile. "Just processing."

She smirked at me before looping her arm through my elbow and tugging me toward the door. I yelped, having no choice but to follow her; for such a tiny thing, she had alarming strength.

Must be a dragon trait...

"You can *process* on the way. Come on! There's so much to see before dinner." Her curls bounced as she whipped her head round, flashing me a grin. "Stavrok wanted you to get the whole tour, and I'm the resident expert."

Cass continued chattering happily as we proceeded down the corridor, and I half-listened, catching glimpses through half-opened doors as we passed. There were a group of women working on a huge tapestry in one room who inclined their heads at the sight of us, and shouts echoed from another room, along with the sound of metal clashing together.

When we got closer, I realized the men were combat training, the way Stavrok had been when I'd confronted him and demanded answers.

It felt like such a long time ago. I was startled to realize that it was only this morning.

"The kitchens are in the basement, and the greenhouses are through there." Cass flung a hand, indicating a high archway at the end of the walkway we stood on. "We grow our own produce. Any surplus is donated to the townsfolk."

I craned my neck over the ledge of the huge glass window, gazing down into the valley that lay below the castle. The town looked tiny from here, the little houses and shops like toys.

"It's so..." I struggled to think of the right word. "Old fashioned?"

Cass giggled. "I guess it must seem that way to you, but we have our technological advances, same as your world. Have you ever been to Chicago? I spent a summer there once—"

I cut her off, remembering my request from earlier. "Speaking of technology, did Stavrok mention anything about a computer to you? I need to send some emails and check in on a couple of things."

Understatement of the century.

With any luck, I hadn't been gone long enough to raise any alarm bells.

Cass gave a heavy sigh. "I'm afraid the Wi-Fi kind of sucks here, but the east tower has a couple of hotspots. We have a small office space next to the library. You can use my laptop if you like."

"Perfect." I grinned.

"Can I show you the greenhouses first?" Cass drew her eyebrows together, eyes wide.

She looked so hopeful that I found myself softening.

"Fine," I said.

The greenhouses were beautiful, built into the center of the castle's intricate roof system and therefore sheltered from the strong winds of the rocky cliff faces on either side. The roof was paneled with multicolored glass, which dappled the floor with prismatic patterns.

After letting Cass show me the grapevines which produced the sweet wine I'd had at breakfast, the fragrant hothouse flowers, and the sunken pool where huge koi fish swam in and out of waterlilies, I finally turned to her with a sigh.

"It's gorgeous, but I *really* need..."

Cass threw her arm around my shoulders and steered me to the door. "I know, I know. I'll take you to your precious computer."

Her scrunched-up face made me chuckle; she reminded me of the face my toddlers made when I took away their crayons.

"Thank you for the tour, Cass," I said. It *was* useful to have a mental map of this place, after all. "Whoever built this place was really onto something."

I glanced back at the beautiful, bright hothouse flowers as we exited the greenhouse, breathing in their dizzying scent one last time. The place was like a little bubble of happiness, a pocket of summer hidden away in this icy, wintery landscape.

"I take it your ancestors put all this together?" I turned to her as we wandered back down the covered walkway, heading for the entrance hall.

She nodded.

"Back there, though?" She pointed toward the greenhouses. "Stavrok built all that."

My heart skipped a beat or two. "Really?"

She grinned, looking as if she could read my train of thought. "It's been a personal project of his for years. He spends time in there still when he can spare it. Self-sufficiency is very important to him."

I struggled to square my image of Stavrok—stoic, strong, the pinnacle of masculinity—with the leafy oasis at the heart of the castle. Still, I knew that first impressions didn't count for everything.

Maybe there was more to him than met the eye.

Cass was watching me carefully. "I know our ways must seem strange to you, Lucy. The human world is a far cry from ours."

We passed through another corridor, one with doors that opened into a large hallway where people sat along long tables, chattering as they worked.

When I looked askance at Cass, she smiled softly. "Everyone in this place plays a part, Lucy. Our kingdom is run, not by dominance and fear like some of the other kingdoms, but by understanding. Stavrok protects everyone, gives them the chance to hone their skills." She pointed to an old woman who spun thread on a giant spindle, while a young girl watched her closely. "They provide for us and themselves, and the kingdom prospers. In return, he will defend us to his dying breath."

I gazed at the scene, lost in thought.

This was what Stavrok was offering me.

A world where I could flourish, and nurture those around me.

Where I could be safe. Where our children would grow up, happy and loved.

I swallowed. "You say that like... it's different here."

She took my arm again, and we continued walking. "I guess it is. Stavrok can be fearsome, but there are parts of this world where true darkness lingers."

Cass bit her lip. It was strange to watch her mood change. The happy, cheery young woman from before disappeared in front of me, like a shadow passing over the sun.

"What do you mean, darkness?" I asked.

I thought about what she had said before. *Dominance and fear.*

Clearly, those other kingdoms Cass mentioned didn't run on the same playbook that Stavrok and his people did here.

"King Magnik rules the kingdom nearest to ours." Cass frowned out of a window as we passed it, like the man himself might suddenly appear. "He's a tyrant. He only cares about wealth and power, and his people suffer for it."

I was silent. My heart hammered as I thought about having to come face to face with such a man in the future. If I stayed with Stavrok, surely I'd need to see him at some point.

After all, what did I have to protect myself if I needed to? No magical powers, no mysterious shapeshifting ability. I was just an ordinary human.

Cass must have seen my face, because she nudged her shoulder into mine. "Hey, don't worry about that now. C'mon, we're almost there!"

I wanted to get her to tell me more about the kingdoms, about how things were done around here, but I forced myself to focus.

One thing at a time.

She led me into a gigantic library, full of floor-to-ceiling bookcases. We wove through the shelves, and I gaped up at the ornate gilded books that lined every wall. A spiral staircase in the corner led up to a small balcony, and through another door we came upon a smaller anteroom, complete with a desk, office supplies, and—

Bingo!

I made a beeline for the computer that sat on a small desk in the corner of the room, and Cass giggled.

"It should be all set up for you," she said. "Give me a shout if you have any problems, yeah? I'll be right outside."

I threw her a smile, grateful for the chance to be alone with my thoughts for the time being.

I opened my email and began to scan my inbox.

My depressingly empty inbox.

I had one unanswered email from the day-care center, asking me if I was sick. It wasn't like me to just not show up for work, and I detected a note of worry in the message underneath the polite annoyance.

I thought hard about what Stavrok had said. I knew the impromptu vacation excuse wouldn't cut it, but...

I began to type, my fingers flying across the keyboard. The more I typed, the more I thought about my life back home.

What I would be returning to, once I got out of here.

The small house, where I lived alone. My day job, where I cared for other people's children. The occasional drink I treated myself to, down at my small town's only bar. Spending the night getting hit on by guys who were only after one thing.

Rinse, and repeat.

Laying out the facts, it made for a pretty bleak existence.

Not that it was all bad. I liked my job well enough. I got on with my colleagues. I saw my parents every week or so.

It was all perfectly... fine.

I looked at the message I'd written, a simple, short email explaining that I had been taken ill suddenly. It didn't sound that convincing, but I hit send anyway.

I thought again about Stavrok. About the way he talked, offering to lay the world at my feet if that was what it took to get me to stay.

I had to admit it; there was something charming about his unwavering belief in me. His certainty that the fates had brought us together, and he wanted to build a life with me.

Granted, if a guy back home had told me he would father my children after only one night together, I would have turned tail and run.

But this wasn't my home.

The rules were different here.

Every time I thought I was beginning to understand them, something new came along and turned everything on its head.

I had to keep my wits about me. But it seemed like the longer I stayed here, the deeper down the rabbit hole I fell.

FOURTEEN

STAVROK

I looked over the perfectly set table. The candles were in place, and all the silverware was laid out precisely.

Normally, I didn't care about such things, but now…

Now I had someone to impress.

The double doors at the other end of the dining room opened a crack, and I straightened my spine, hands behind my back. I had elected to wear a simple navy shirt and slacks for tonight's meal: a nice halfway point between my training gear and the formalwear my advisors forced me into for diplomatic visits.

The door slid open, and Lucy slipped into the room. My heart lightened upon seeing her. She wore a simple low-necked dress, and her long hair flowed loose around her shoulders.

It was thrilling to see her embrace the fashions of the land so readily. She already looked like she belonged here. She looked like a queen.

My queen.

Her lips quirked upwards when she caught my eye, and she hurried over to meet me.

"Your Majesty," she said, giving me a small curtsey and giggling in a way that made me smile.

"My queen," I replied, giving her a bow in turn.

She scrunched up her face and waved away my remark, but she accepted the chair I pulled out for her without fuss. The woman was a conundrum. A delightful puzzle that I couldn't wait to spend the rest of my life figuring out.

Our food was brought in, and we began to eat in a comfortable silence. I surveyed her over the top of my wineglass, smiling at the way she flushed when she caught my eyes on her.

"This color suits you." I stroked a hand along her ruby red sleeve. "You should order more styles in this palette. You make a pleasing picture."

"Is that so?" she said, raising an eyebrow at me, but I could tell she wasn't angry at my remark.

On the contrary, she looked strangely shy. As if she wasn't used to men complimenting her in this way. I couldn't fathom the motivations of human men. To me, she was a feast for the eyes.

"I trust your day was pleasing?" I said, taking a bite of tender lamb shank and eyeing her.

She nodded. "Your cousin's fun."

"Cass." I smiled warmly. "I'm glad you like her. She's like a little sister to me—talkative, and always underfoot, but she means well. I hope she showed you all this place has to offer."

"She did." Lucy met my gaze, her tone careful. "I got the works."

"Good." I clinked my glass against hers. I wasn't hiding the fact that I wanted her to stay with me, after all. "Did you find the computer you requested?"

"I did, thank you." She cast her eyes downward, fiddling with her dessert fork. "I've tied up all the loose ends. So, I'm all yours—"

I grinned at her, and she snorted.

"For now." She pointed her fork at me, before taking another bite of lamb and groaning. "God, the food here is amazing."

"Care to join me for dessert?" I said, lowering my voice a shade.

She held my gaze. Her beauty was highlighted this evening, bathed by the candlelight's warm glow. She bit her plump lip, and it grew redder and fuller.

"Of course."

In due course, the strawberries were brought out, but I found myself watching her more than anything else. She dipped them in melted chocolate and brought them to her mouth, her eyelashes fluttering with pleasure at the taste.

Despite the servants standing by watching us, lust began to weave through my blood stream.

A drizzle of chocolate coated her little finger, and I couldn't help but take her hand and pull her finger toward my lips. I trailed my tongue over her flesh, and in answer she took a sharp intake of breath.

My heated gaze met hers.

Her pupils were large, and her flushed chest was rising and falling a little more rapidly than before. I let her hand fall to the table and leaned in closer, sliding my hand up the outside of her thigh.

She shoved away from the table, her chair scraping back as she stood up abruptly. Half a strawberry tumbled from her fingers, but she ignored it.

"I'm tired," she said, biting her words out. "It's been a long day."

I frowned. She clearly desired me just as much as I wanted her.

Something was holding her back.

"I'll take you to my bedchamber," I said, keeping my voice low.

I didn't understand how the mood of the evening had turned so quickly. I wanted to take her again. My dragon demanded its mate, roaring with frustration.

It would only be satisfied when Lucy and I were both sated and exhausted, but apparently my advances were unwelcome tonight.

"I want my own, uh, chamber." Lucy crossed her arms, staring me down. "You said I could have anything I wanted, right? I want this."

I gaped at her.

No woman had ever spoken to me in such a manner before.

It only made me want her more. She wasn't afraid of me at all, this small human woman.

I knew, in that moment, that I would level cities in order to keep her safe.

I also knew that we should be apart right now.

She wanted some space, and my baser urges were howling for me to throw her against the table and ravage her.

It was only a matter of time before one of these eventualities would prevail.

"Very well," I said, keeping my voice impassive. I gestured to a nearby servant, who sprang to attention. "See to it that my mate has everything she needs for the night."

Lucy turned to go, but before she could pull away completely, I took her hand in mine.

"Sleep well, dear one," I murmured, pressing my lips to the back of her hand.

Just before she withdrew it and walked out of the dining hall, I swore I felt her fingertips brush, light as a feather, against my cheek.

An hour later I found myself alone in my bedchamber, staring up at the ceiling.

I had spent my whole life in this bed, alone or in the company of an endless number of heartless women.

It had never bothered me. I always slept a deep, untroubled sleep, or spent my nights in the arms of a conquest.

Now the frustration itched under my skin. I ached for release, but I had nowhere to turn.

The one thing that would sate my burning desire was in the castle, tantalizingly close, but just out of reach. I buried my face in my pillow and groaned aloud, praying for sleep to come and put an end to my suffering.

Sleep did not come.

Instead, there was a knock at the door.

Hope flared in my chest, and I sat up, knocking my bedclothes aside.

She'd come back to me.

"Enter," I called, trying to keep the need out of my voice but hearing it anyway.

A figure entered the room, and my heart sank into my stomach.

"Majesty." The woman in the doorway gave a deep curtsey. "I came to make sure you were all right."

It was the maidservant Daisy, was it? No, Daphne.

"I'm fine," I said, dropping back onto my bed with a sigh. "I take it Lucy is settled?"

"She is, sire." Daphne edged the door shut behind her.

I cracked an eye open to watch her as she approached my bed.

"I was just wondering whether you required any other services before I departed for the night." Her hands came up to loosen the lacings at the front of her dress. "I could please you, if you wish it."

I eyed her, a wave of exhaustion crashing over me.

She was pretty. Her long black hair was fastened in a braid, and her brown eyes were fringed with long lashes.

In bygone days, I wouldn't have thought twice before pulling her into bed with me.

I'd had many beautiful women, including this one before me, but they were pale shadows to me now.

I looked at Daphne, and all I felt was emptiness. A longing for the touch of someone else. I knew in that moment that I would never have another woman again.

"Please." I passed a hand over my face, waving her away. "Leave me."

There was a small noise, like an inhale. Of shock, maybe. Perhaps the girl hadn't been expecting me to reject her so easily.

Tough. Things were different.

I'd found my mate now. I knew what true pleasure looked like, a real, deep intimacy that was already blooming into love.

I didn't hear her leave.

Sleep pulled me under like a tidal wave, and I succumbed to it with open arms. Tomorrow I would win back my queen. I wanted nothing more to do with any other woman, ever again.

Lucy

I woke up to what I thought was the sound of birdsong outside my window. I lay in the pale morning light with my eyes closed, coming to my senses.

As I regained consciousness, I realized the sound wasn't birds; it was the high, piercing sound of the icy winds that wrapped around the castle walls. I wasn't in my bed at home. The room I slept in was huge and high-ceilinged, and the silk sheets pooled around me where I lay in the center of a vast four-poster bed.

Memories of the night before flooded me, and I groaned,

squeezing my eyes shut tight and sinking down underneath the covers.

I couldn't pretend any more. This wasn't a dream. This was my life.

I pushed the bedclothes back and shifted to the edge of the mattress, wincing when my bare feet touched the cold flagstones.

There were no clocks in the room, but judging by the dim light and the silence that surrounded me, it was still early.

I padded over to the empty fireplace and smiled as my feet sank into the lush rug that stretched in front of it. I traced the edge of the dragon woven into the center of the rug and sighed.

My night had been spent tossing and turning. The bed had been too big, too cold.

The memory of Stavrok's body curled up against mine, his heat, the safety I felt in his arms—it was too much. My body hummed with the knowledge that he was somewhere within the walls of the castle.

I craved him by my side, even after one day.

Walking away from him last night had been the hardest thing I'd ever done. I'd wanted nothing more than to melt into his touch, to open myself to him again. From the fire in his eyes, I could tell he felt the same way.

But I'd resolved to be cautious.

My judgement was already out the window. I didn't need another crazy, intense night to scramble my brain further.

When Stavrok was around, it was impossible to think rationally about anything. I refused to be a captive here; if I was going to stay, it would be *my* decision.

The stone walls that surrounded me were suddenly suffocating.

I turned and reached for the layers I had discarded last night on the chair beside my bed, dressing myself quickly. At this hour, a chill permeated the air, and I was glad for the soft fur against my skin. Toeing on my shoes, I headed out the door before I could overanalyze my actions.

With no particular direction in mind, I found myself wandering down the castle hallways.

My head ached as I thought about everything I'd learned yesterday. About the town, its people. About the things Cass told me: Stavrok's vision for his kingdom.

For all the years of his rule, he'd been by himself. It humbled me, knowing how much he'd built, all on his own.

It was easier than it should've been to imagine myself by his side.

There were things I could help with. I'd spent my entire adult life working with children, hadn't I? There had to be plenty of projects to run, lessons to teach. I could do so much... I was sure of it.

In my mind's eye, I could see us, five or ten years from now, surrounded by our friends. Our servants. Keeping them safe from those who would threaten us.

The image expanded. I saw us surrounded by children.

Our children, running down the staircase in the great hall, playing together, swinging between our joined hands as we walked through these hallways.

My heart swelled.

Stavrok wanted me to be his queen. If I stayed, I would have a man who wanted me, just as I was.

Who didn't think I was too fat to be beautiful.

In his eyes, I was perfect.

I'd never have that at home, in my little town with narrow-minded men.

I was so caught up that I barely noticed the figure watching me at the foot of the stairs, and I almost walked into her.

"Oof!" I reached out a hand, steadying myself.

"Oh, I'm sorry, miss."

My eyes focused, and I exhaled heavily, shaking my head at the maid who stood in my path.

"No worries! My fault." I smiled.

The maid smiled back, but there was something guarded in her eyes.

Right. I was still a stranger in these lands. It would naturally take a while for its people to warm up to me.

Still, what was the harm in testing the waters?

"What's your name?" I asked, feeling a bit foolish.

I was probably distracting this girl from her chores for the sake of a little light conversation.

"Daphne, miss." The girl's eyes flicked up and down, and she bobbed a curtsey. A strange smile played at the corners of her mouth.

I already regretted starting the conversation, but I pressed on. "Have you been working here long, Daphne?"

She straightened her shoulders and flicked her hair back. She was pretty, like all the women were here, with her long hair and dark eyes. "The castle isn't my workplace. It's my home."

"Of course."

I'd put my foot in it, somehow, but in what way I didn't know.

Daphne took a neat step forward, looking me directly in the eye. "I'm not some naïve newcomer, miss. I'm devoted to my life here, just as I am devoted to the king."

I nodded, lowering my gaze. "I understand. I didn't mean—"

"I took care of the king's appetites last night," Daphne whispered.

My stomach swooped sickeningly.

She went on. "I consider it an honor to leave him well satisfied. I suggest if you can't keep up with our king's needs, human, you should fly off back to where you came from and leave him to those who can."

I stepped back. My hands clenched into fists. I wanted to slap the smug look off her face, but I managed to control myself, taking short, sharp breaths as I struggled to regain my composure.

Daphne's face settled into a placid smile. "Will that be all, miss?"

I was trembling with anger, but I knew when I was beaten.

The people here would never accept me. I wasn't one of them, and I never would be.

The women would hate me for being an outsider, for being the one to lay claim to their king after all these years.

The unfairness of it screamed out at me.

It wasn't my choice. Stavrok had found *me*, chosen *me*, brought *me* here to rule by his side.

But you claimed him too, a small voice said in the back of my mind. *He's yours now, fate or no fate. Everyone can see it.*

Apparently, fate had a twisted sense of humor.

I'd screwed up any chance I'd had of making things work between us. I'd driven him into the arms of another woman.

I gave her a short nod, and she turned tail, leaving me standing at the foot of the staircase with a swirling mind and a heart that was, despite all my best efforts, broken.

FIFTEEN

I only wanted one thing: to hide.

The trouble was, I still didn't know the castle and all its hiding places well enough. Every time I ended up in some corner or other, a guard or servant wandered into the vicinity and looked at me like I was crazy.

Eventually I settled for prowling through the great hall before making my way to the dining room.

My blood was up, and there was nothing I could do to stop the rage that pooled in my stomach when I thought about my so-called "fated mate".

I prickled with frustration, pacing up and down in front of the roaring fireplace. The staff shot me nervous looks, but I ignored them. There was only one person I wanted to see.

When the man himself finally appeared, I had worked myself up into an anger that threatened to crack the very floor beneath my feet.

Stavrok was about to find out that this human woman had enough of a temper to take on a dragon.

He closed the door behind him and stepped into the room. I

drew in a sharp intake of breath. He was pale and there were dark shadows under his eyes.

Maybe he'd slept as badly as I had.

Or maybe he's been up all night fucking other women.

When I met his gaze, his demeanor changed. He straightened up, and his face softened, a spark of hope shining in his eyes.

I met his eyes and kept my expression stony.

He'd brought me here, into his life, his world. And he wasn't going to take me for a fool.

"Good morning, dear one." He ventured closer, coming to a standstill about two feet away from me. "Did you have a restful night?"

I folded my arms. A hot pulse of irritation flooded through me at the way his eyes dropped to my chest. Folding my arms had pushed up my generous cleavage. I huffed and uncrossed them.

Men!

"Not really," I said shortly.

"I'm sorry to hear it." He moved closer, reaching out to touch my shoulder. "I missed you in my bed last night."

I pushed his hand off me and stepped back, narrowing my eyes. He actually sounded *regretful,* like he meant it. The audacity of his behavior threw me off my game a little, but I recovered myself.

"Did you?" I smoldered up at him, and he frowned, like I'd unbalanced him. *Good.* "Did you miss me, my *king?*"

"More than you can know," he replied, before tilting his head. "Lucy, is everything... all right? You seem agitated."

"There's no point in keeping up the charade, Stavrok," I snapped. "I know everything."

He scrunched up his face, which only sought to enrage me further.

He must think I'm a complete idiot!

"I ran into Daphne this morning." I let the words out in a rush of breath, relieved to finally release what I'd been holding back. "She told me what happened last night."

His gaze darkened, and I felt vindication sing through my veins.

Finally, we're going to have this out.

"The maidservant?"

"I can't believe I was actually starting to believe all the *bullshit* you fed me," I said. "All that crap about fate bringing us together —and *then,* the minute my back is turned, you go off and fuck the first willing woman you come across!"

Stavrok's mouth dropped open.

Dragon or no dragon, I was more than a match for this giant of a man.

"Lucy," he said, his shoulders squared off and taut with tension. "I have no idea what you're talking about."

"Is that how it is here?" I asked. A part of me thrilled at the heat building up between us. I wanted more of it. I wanted to stoke the flames until the inferno couldn't be contained any more. "You fuck other women whenever you please? What exactly am I here for, Stavrok? To give you heirs while you take your pleasures elsewhere?"

I pressed a hand to my stomach, feeling a wave of *something* pass through me.

I continued on, undeterred.

"You must think I'm an idiot." I gave a hollow laugh. "Well, I might not be anything special—I might not be a *magical shapeshifter*—but I know when I'm being played."

"You think I took Daphne to bed last night?" Stavrok's voice had dropped so low, I could feel it in my chest, even from this distance. "Lucy, I slept *alone.* She offered herself to me, yes, but I—"

"There it is!" I cut him off. "Finally."

I took a perverse kind of pleasure in getting the truth out of him like this, bit by bit. It was like touching a wound that hadn't healed yet. I couldn't stop the pain, but I liked being the one in control of it.

"Nothing happened!" Stavrok said, his voice booming off the walls. "Whatever she told you, it's a falsehood! I want no woman but you, Lucy."

I scoffed, but tears pricked my eyes. I dashed them away. On some level, I knew this rejection was going to happen. Maybe it was better it happened sooner rather than later.

A man like this—strong, handsome, virile—what did he want with a woman like me?

He could have anyone he wanted. He was the kind of man that beautiful women threw themselves at on a daily basis.

I swallowed around the lump in my throat. "I don't believe you!"

"What would you have me do to prove it to you?" he asked. "Have I not already offered you everything I have? Have I not laid it out at your feet, from the moment we first met?"

I shoved down the small piece of doubt that threatened to crack through my defences and took a step toward him.

"If it's not this one, it'll be another! Sooner or later, you'll see—"

"See what?"

"How much you're missing!" I said, running my hands through my hair so that it tumbled loosely around my shoulders. "The women here—I can't give you the things that they can! I'm not a shifter, I'm not beautiful. I'm not enough for you! You should never have taken me, Stavrok, because now I'll always know what it's supposed to feel like!"

I rushed forward and pushed at his chest with my fists. I gasped as he caught my wrists in his large hands and tugged me forwards until I curved into his body.

"I'll always know how it's meant to be between two people, and I'll *never* feel like this again! You've *ruined* me!"

He snarled, his eyes flashing. In the depths of his gaze, I caught a glimmer of the dragon that slumbered inside of the king.

Stavrok's hands tightened around my wrists, and his thunderous expression morphed into something deeper, raw and urgent. Lust raced through my veins as he pressed up against me, backing me into the wall and holding me there with ease.

"If you don't believe me," his said, his voice shooting through me, low and dangerous, "I'll have to show you."

I groaned and sank back. Anger and adrenaline pulsed through me, but it was impossible to keep up the fight when he had me pinned against the wall. I was surrounded by him. His skin pulsed with heat, and his fingers shifted and flexed against my wrists.

He must have felt my heartbeat fluttering just beneath the surface of my skin, because his eyes flicked upwards, assessing my ragged breaths, the way my chest rose and fell, the flush that spread out from my décolletage.

"Yes." The word tripped out of me, unbidden, and his eyes narrowed.

He dropped my wrists and his hands fell below my waist, pulling up my skirts with an urgency that I hadn't seen from him before. He hitched my legs up until he had me braced against the wall. My eyes rolled back, and I groaned, trying to pull him even closer.

The thin layers of fabric that separated us were torturous. I longed to feel his hot skin against mine, feel every inch of him pressed up against my body, but I had to settle for what I could reach. My hands dragged over his perfect torso, and his forehead pushed up against mine as he tore away the last of my underclothes, leaving nothing between us.

If I wasn't half-crazy with desire I would've chuckled.

So many layers, so little time.

I felt his fingers, blunt and insistent, against my entrance, and I shivered. He grunted, satisfied to find me slick and ready. I ached, the sense of emptiness overwhelming me.

I need him inside me.

I hooked my ankles against his hips and pulled, no longer caring about self-restraint or decorum, or the fact that we were in a public place where anyone might walk in on us.

All I cared about was this. I needed him to fuck me until neither of us could see straight.

His mouth found my neck, and he bit down as he sank into me. I wriggled, trapped between the wall and his hot, insistent body.

It was overwhelming, dizzying. Perfect.

He began to thrust, and I sobbed, fisting my hand into his hair and drumming my heels against his back in a silent plea for him to move faster, deeper.

He obliged, pounding into me relentlessly, and before long I felt myself start to tighten around his cock. My orgasm slammed into me, wave after wave of bliss rippling through my body, and I whimpered as his onslaught only increased in pace.

My whimpers tightened my throat. I murmured to him, high and breathy.

"Stavrok... please... I need you..."

He snarled, dropping his head to my shoulder as he continued to thrust.

"Mine," he breathed. "You're *mine.*"

"I'm yours," I said, and I opened my mouth, readily accepting his bruising kiss.

His thrusts began to grow less precise; something baser, more primal, took over. His grip on my hips grew firmer, and he began pulling down my hips as he hitched himself up to meet me, as if I were nothing more to him than an instrument for his pleasure. I moaned at the thought, at the way his breathing shifted, at the feeling of his thighs tensing up.

He spilled into me, and the feeling of his seed pulsing deep inside sent me over the edge again.

Little by little, our breathing returned to normal. The sound of it echoed loudly through the silent dining hall.

Slowly, inch by inch, he released me, and I trembled as I slid down from the wall, my hands reaching to adjust my skirt.

My legs felt like jelly, and my head spun. I stumbled, and his broad hand caught my elbow.

I looked up at him, and he looked down at me.

I couldn't know for sure, but I was willing to bet that our expressions were mirror images of one another.

There was only one feeling that raced through my mind, over and over, building until it could be encapsulated in a single expression.

Oh. Fuck.

It wasn't that I was falling for him.

I've already fallen.

G olden sunlight streamed in through the window. I stretched, eyes still half-closed, and reached out a hand. A smile grew on my face when my fingers brushed up against the form, warm and solid, curled up beside me.

Lucy.

I had worried the previous day had been an illusion. A fever dream, of sorts, conjured up by my fractured brain to mask the pain of my mate rejecting me.

It appeared not.

The real thing lay beside me, golden hair splayed out over the pillow. One hand curled upwards beside her slumbering face, and I couldn't resist brushing those soft fingers, watching her hand twitch and her eyelashes flutter.

She looked like a princess, straight out of the stories my mother used to read to me as a child.

Her gorgeous green eyes opened, and her lovely features softened when she saw me. Sleepily, she raised a hand up to push a lock of hair off my brow. At the gentleness of her touch, I bowed my head, pressing a kiss into her outstretched palm.

"What a gentleman." She giggled. "Good morning."

"It is indeed," I murmured, pressing myself up against her side and combing my fingers through her hair, enjoying the soft texture.

She snuggled closer. I was gratified by the contact and pleased at the assurance of the motion. She had no problem dragging my free arm tight around her waist, and I growled in satisfaction as I traced a hand over the curve of her waist.

"What are your plans today?" Lucy whispered, pressing a kiss into my neck.

I stroked her arm absently, thinking. "Matters of state, a few meetings this afternoon. Nothing urgent."

She hummed approval and nuzzled into my neck. I wondered if the scratchiness of my stubble bothered her, but I didn't voice the thought. I was enjoying her kisses too much.

"Besides," I murmured, running a hand up her spine, "my advisors will understand. I've found my fated mate, after all these years. It's a cause for celebration."

There was a long silence.

I frowned. Lucy's back had grown tense at my words, and her body withdrew from mine under the bedcovers.

"Fated mates." She didn't turn her head, and her voice was quiet, but I was hanging on to every word. "You really believe in that stuff, don't you?"

My frown deepened. I pulled my arms back, and she flipped onto her back, staring up at me with a blank expression.

"Of course," I said, puzzled. "You feel it, don't you? The pull toward me, our connection? Don't talk of it as if..."

"As if what?"

"As if it's some"—I cast out a hand, struggling for the words —"fairy tale. I assure you, what's passed between us is real. It is a bond that cannot be broken. Neither time nor distance will weaken its power."

She pressed her lips together. The thin line of them grew white, and my anger bubbled to the surface.

"You *know* this." I growled. "I know you can feel it too, Lucy."

"Don't tell me what I feel," she snapped, and my stomach dropped. She pushed the bedsheets back, climbed out of bed, and grabbed a robe from my coat rack. "I *feel* like this is a load of shit, if you must know."

"What do you mean?"

I clambered to my feet, mirroring her movements. She had already circled the bed and walked out of reach. I resisted the urge to pace after her, sensing that it would only escalate things.

Escalate what? *We were having a pleasant conversation five minutes ago.*

The mood had changed so fast I had whiplash.

She rounded on me. Even though I stood a head taller than her, I backed up a couple of steps at the force of her glare.

"I mean, you promised me *time*," she said. "You promised me I could go home if I wanted to!"

"And I'll honor that promise!"

My heart hammered in my chest, and the blood rushed through my eardrums. *She wants to leave me.*

I couldn't believe it. I'd never heard of such a thing happening before. When a dragon shifter found their fated mate, that was it. They were bonded for life.

I swallowed.

Maybe it was because she was human. I should have known that crucial difference between us would come back to haunt me.

She stared at me, her face pale and her eyes flashing. Belatedly, I realized I had been yelling.

At length, she drew herself up to her full height and looked me square in the face, shoulders back. She was regal. She may not have been born into it, but she was certainly a queen in my eyes.

"I'm going for a shower," she said, her voice trembling with repressed emotion. "Alone."

Before I had a chance to respond, she turned and strode into the bathroom, slamming the door shut behind her. A few moments later, the water turned on.

I resisted the urge to release my dragon then and there. Love and rage warred within my chest. I wanted to scorch a forest to the ground, level fields and raze valleys in my fury.

Instead, I turned on my heel and walked out of the bedchamber.

It was time for a sparring session.

Whoever I was training with today, I didn't envy them one bit.

~

Lucy

By the time I climbed out of the shower, my skin was flushed and pruney, and my ire had cooled considerably. As I towelled off my hair, I cast a nervous glance at the door that led to the bedchamber.

The shower had washed away my prickling frustration, but I wasn't ready to face Stavrok yet.

When I pushed open the door, I revealed an empty room. The bed was neatly made, but there was no sign of the king anywhere.

My heart sank, caught somewhere between relief and sadness.

Ugh. I need to walk and clear my head. This place is driving me crazy.

I slipped on a simple velvet dress and, after a moment of hesitation, a fur mantle that I found hanging in the vast wardrobe.

It was fancier than anything I owned back home, but it was soft and warm.

I smoothed the fur around my shoulders, turning to assess myself in the mirror.

A knock at my door.

"Lucy? Are you awake yet?"

I smiled to myself. "Yep! Come in, Cass."

The door creaked open, and Cass slipped inside. She bounded over to me and bobbed up behind my shoulder. She grinned at me in the mirror, and I managed to smile back.

"The royal furs," she said. "It suits you!"

I let out a groan of dismay, and her brow furrowed. The gesture reminded me of Stavrok, and my mood sank even further.

"Oh, no!" She bit her lip, eyes wide. "What's wrong?"

I took her arm, shaking my head, lost for words. *Where to even begin.*

"I'm going for a walk." I led her to the doorway, out into the corridor. "And you're coming with me."

"Okay..." Cass's voice trailed after me as I strode down the corridor, not bothering to slow my pace for her. She trotted after me, panting. "Do I get to ask what this is about, or...?"

I shook my head, hurtling down the wide staircase and rounding the corner.

I was kind of impressed with myself. I knew the layout of this place like I'd lived here for years.

Like it's already home to me.

I forced the traitorous thought out of my mind and forced open the double doors, making for the outdoor walkway Cass had shown me a couple of days ago.

Air. That was what I needed. Fresh air, to clear away the storms swirling in my head.

"Lucy!" Cass burst through the doorway in a flurry of chestnut curls, laying a hand on my arm. "Tell me what's going on already!"

At her touch, I deflated, pulling back until we were walking side by side. I took a deep breath of the cool air, and exhaled, long and slow.

I started feeling better just for being outside.

"This is all happening so..." I flailed. "It's a *lot*, okay, and I'm... A week ago, I was living a totally normal life in my totally normal town, and suddenly, overnight, I'm the *soulmate* of a *king*—"

"Slow down..." Cass interjected, but I couldn't stop.

I always got like this when I was angry or upset. Once the words started, they kept on coming, faster and faster.

"He wants me to live in his castle and be his queen, and rule by his side, and have his babies, and—oh, my God." I ran my fingers through my hair, rounding on her. "My kids are going to be dragons, Cass. *Dragons.*"

"Well," Cass said weakly. "They won't be dragons all the time. It's more like... like a part of our souls."

I shot her an incredulous look and kept walking. The wide stone archways we passed through looked out over a snowy vista. A light flurry was falling, coating the castle roofs and turrets with white.

"We're shifters, Lucy." Cass's voice was gentle, reassuring. "And they won't just be his children. They'll be yours, too."

"That's exactly the problem!" I sighed. "You, Stavrok, everyone is talking as if I've already agreed to spend my life here, just because the fates have decided it."

Cass tilted her head to the side as though she was puzzled, so I sighed and tried to explain.

"In my world, there's no such thing as fate, or destiny." I looked out over the beautiful world I'd found myself in. I heard Stavrok's voice echo through my mind. *A world of Fire and Ice.* "I make my own choices, Cass. Nobody else. Not fate. Not even a dragon king."

We were silent for a few more paces. The wind howled around us, and I shivered, drawing my collar up around my neck.

"I hear you," Cass said eventually. "I just..."

She looked up at me, eyes piercing through mine. I felt exposed.

"I can't understand why you would ever want to leave this place," she said. "Or leave Stavrok."

I bit my lip. "I guess it must be kind of hard to wrap your head around, huh?"

Cass laughed. "Yes. If I found my fated mate..." She exhaled, fixing her eyes on the horizon, lost in thought. "I wouldn't ever want to be apart from them, let alone in another world entirely."

I didn't reply. I tried to imagine crossing the border and returning to the human world, starting my life again like none of this had ever happened.

Deep in my stomach, the thought didn't sit right with me.

I didn't want Cass to know that.

I sighed heavily. "Cass, I... I can't be a prisoner here. Whatever I feel for Stavrok, I'm my own person."

Cass opened her mouth to say something, but before she could, there was a tap on my shoulder.

Her eyes slid past mine, widening, and I whirled around to face two tall figures dressed in the livery of the castle guards.

I didn't recognise them.

That fact wouldn't have been unusual in itself—I hadn't been here that long, after all—but from Cass's expression I could tell she didn't know them either.

I straightened my shoulders, trying for an aura of confidence that I didn't feel.

"Yes?"

The one on the left spoke. His voice was low and gravelly. "Ma'am, you have to come with us."

Cass nudged me aside, stepping between me and the newcomers. "Why? Anything you can say to her, you can say to me."

A glow of warmth shot through me, but it vanished when the men's expressions darkened. Their eyes were glowing in a faintly familiar way.

"We were told to make this quiet," the one on the right said. He was shorter than his friend, and his voice had a mean undercurrent. "But we're authorized to use force if necessary."

I shivered, but Cass was getting angrier by the moment. Her brows were furrowed, her fists were clenched, and her face had gone an unhealthy shade of red.

"Authorized by *who?*"

Quick as a flash, the taller of the pair lashed out, swift and merciless. The uppercut sent Cass flying into the stone edge of the walkway. She hit it with a sharp *crack*, and fell to the floor, where she lay, unmoving.

"Cass!" I screamed.

I shot forward, stumbling toward her. She looked so still. I needed to check if she was breathing. She couldn't *possibly* be—

Firm hands grabbed me, and I struggled as I was pulled back, away from her. No matter how much I thrashed, the grip on my arms was as solid and immovable as iron.

"No! Let me go!" I twisted around, desperately casting around for anyone who might be nearby. "*Stavrok!*"

The last thing I saw were a pair of glittering, malevolent eyes, before a cloth was pressed against my nose and mouth.

And then everything went black.

SEVENTEEN

LUCY.

When I woke up, a single feeling slammed into me with inescapable force.

Cold.

I moaned and shuddered, curling into my side and wrapping my arms around myself in a futile attempt to warm up.

I'd been cold since I arrived in the land of Fire and Ice. But for the first time, the real arctic temperatures of this world were hitting me. I'd seen the fire first-hand, and now I was getting the ice.

I inched my eyes open, squinting as my eyes adjusted to the dim light. I was in a cavernous, windowless room. Damp trickled down the stone walls, and a torch flickered in a hollow crevice, casting long shadows over the uneven floor.

I pushed myself up onto my hands, trying to keep my rising panic in check. I was lying on a thin wooden bench pushed up against the wall. There were iron brackets bolted into the stonework just above my head.

Wow, I really don't want to know what those are for.

I curled my legs up beside me on the bench, my eyes flickering back and forth, taking stock of my surroundings from the limited vantage point.

Dark, damp room. Stone walls.

Were those *chains* coiled up in the far corner?

I didn't care to get up and check.

I dropped my head, pressing my cheek against my knees.

It looked like I'd finally made it to the dungeons after all.

A cold, creeping misery swept through my chest, and I groaned.

Had I crossed Stavrok one too many times?

We'd fought badly this morning. Granted, it was just a continuation of the argument from the day before, but still.

He was the king. He must be unused to dealing with the sharp end of a temper like mine.

But to go so far as throwing me in the dungeons over it?

That just didn't square with the picture I had of him. He could be fierce, sure, but he treated me with a deference and respect I was unused to in a man.

Every scrap of evidence I had to go on told me that he was strong and just. A fair, kind leader of his people. I hadn't seen anything to point to the contrary.

A shiver rolled down my spine.

I pressed a hand to my stomach, and a jolt of rage sparked through me. I leapt to my feet, mentally and physically shaking myself out of my stupor.

Come on, Lucy! Get it together.

I began to pace, examining every inch of my prison as I went. A quick assessment told me I was still wearing the clothes I had put on this morning, before going out for my walk with—

Cass.

Whoever had kidnapped me, they had taken out Cass first.

Which suggested that Stavrok wasn't behind this whole thing. He wouldn't hurt Cass. She was family.

I frowned, pivoting on my heel. My hand crept over my stomach again, cradling it.

You may already be pregnant, he'd said.

If Stavrok thought the human world was too dangerous for any potential children I might be carrying, surely throwing me in a dungeon wasn't on the cards, either.

My gaze fell on the heavy oak door, set into the wall on the far side of the room.

I approached it slowly, cautiously, leaned in, and pressed my ear against the wood.

At first, I heard nothing but water dripping and the sound of my own breaths. My breath misted in the air in front of me, reminding me ironically of a dragon puffing smoke.

Damn, it really *was* cold.

Then, I heard voices.

They were faint at first, but they grew louder and louder, like their owners were travelling down the corridor toward me.

"...better be worth it, that's all I'm saying. If Magnik is wrong about her, it could bring our kingdom into open war."

More footsteps. Then, a second voice.

"Our king isn't wrong. She's Stavrok's mate. I know Stavrok—he'll do whatever it takes to get her back."

"Those lands have belonged to his family for generations. Do you really think he'll give them all up over one woman?" The speaker gave a snort. "A *human*, at that?"

"Maybe one day you'll find your fated mate, Tristan."

There was a grunt of protest, like someone just got elbowed in the ribs.

"Till then, you should keep your trap shut about it."

"Oh, yeah? Maybe Elsie's tired of you. I could swing by your house later, find out if you can have more than one soulmate... Ouch!"

The voices were moving off now, growing fainter. I waited, my body tense, but they passed right by my door without stopping.

My mind raced. The name Magnik was so familiar to me. Where had I heard it before? Wherever I was, it wasn't Stavrok's kingdom.

My stomach filled with ice. I was in enemy territory. And I was being used as a bargaining chip. All over some *land.*

I burned hot with rage and embarrassment. They hadn't even bothered to tie me up; to them, I was just a powerless human, a pawn to move around as they played their political games.

I watched my lonely flame flickering, casting strange shadows against the ancient stonework. Something curled in my stomach, something that made me stagger over to the bench and sit heavily. I sank my head into my hands.

It was a new sensation, something I hadn't felt since arriving here.

Dread.

~

Stavrok

I SPENT the morning working out my frustration in the courtyard.

The familiar, heavy clash of metal against metal, the adrenaline pounding through my veins, the satisfaction of besting our strongest fighters—all of it soothed me, and by mid-morning I found that my temper had cooled.

I waved off my sparring partner, standing alone in the center of the courtyard and staring up at the sky.

It was a cold, bright day, and I inhaled deep lungfuls of the fresh mountain air before stooping to pick up a water jug and gulping gratefully.

The fight had cleared my head, like it always did.

As I wiped down with a spare towel, my thoughts turned to the events of the morning.

Already I regretted the way things had gone with Lucy. I should've calmed her, the way only a soulmate could.

It seemed that I couldn't help myself with her. When we fought, all the adrenaline I had as a warrior sprang to the fore, mixed in with a hot, tantalising undercurrent of lust.

Lust which she met in equal force, every single time.

Our bond was a powder keg, and I kept lighting the fuse.

My limbs shifted, restless. My sparring practice had taken the edge off my frustration, but already the need for her was beginning to creep back in.

My mind was made up.

I pivoted on my heel, heading for the stairwell. I would track her down, and we could work through our heated feelings together—preferably up against a wall somewhere, or in our bathroom tub.

A shudder of anticipation ran through me, and a smile ghosted across my face.

Before I reached the stairs, a shout echoed from across the yard.

"Majesty!"

I scowled, not wanting to abandon my new mission.

"Yes, what is it?" I turned around.

James strode up to me. He was breathing heavily, like he had been running.

"Quickly," I said. "I have urgent business to attend to."

"Not as urgent as this." James brandished a letter, holding it out to me.

I wanted to brush him off, but there was an unfamiliar worry in his face that gave me pause. My eyes narrowed. I took the letter and opened it.

· · ·

STAVROK —

I WANT to see which you value more: that goldmine of minerals you refuse to part with, or your precious soulmate.

Here is my offer. If you give up your lands to me, I will ensure your new queen is returned to you, alive and unharmed.

If not... I'm afraid that I can't be certain of her safety.

THINK IT OVER.

Magnik

I READ THE WORDS CAREFULLY.

Then I read them again.

My brain refused to believe it. My queen, my love, my soulmate... held for ransom over some petty political argument.

I had never trusted Magnik, but even for him, this was beyond the pale.

The depth of the betrayal shook me to my core. Rage unlike anything I'd ever known, screaming inside my mind. My anger was so potent, I was surprised it didn't crack the stones beneath my feet. I let out a roar and shredded the letter, leaving the pieces to flutter to the ground.

James's face was pale and set, his mouth pressed into a thin line.

"What is this?" My voice boomed over the entire courtyard. "Where is she? Where is Lucy?"

People had begun to trickle into the courtyard, presumably to find out where all the noise was coming from.

"Sire, please," James said, "you must calm yourself." My vision was distorting, my muscles clenching. My dragon was waking up. I growled, and James backed up a couple of steps, wide-eyed.

With difficulty, I shoved my dragon shifter back down again. It could do me no good right now. I needed to be able to talk.

"I'm very far from calm. Tell me everything."

"Majesty," someone called out, pushing through the small gathering of people.

They grumbled and moved aside for her, and a small pathway formed through the sea of bodies.

My eyes narrowed as I caught sight of the strange procession of people.

The voice belonged to Maddie. She was leading a group of court officials through the crowd.

Their long robes clustered protectively around a slight figure, who was walking with the aid of two guards. I caught a flash of curly hair, and a fresh jolt of panic spiked through my chest.

"Cass?"

I rushed forward, jostling a guard out of the way as I took her by the elbow. My little cousin was ashen pale, and to my horror, there was a dark smear of blood at her temple.

In spite of her obvious wooziness, she shot me a weak smile. "Hey, Stavrok."

"What happened?"

Her large eyes fixed on mine. Her usual bouncy energy was gone, replaced by a stark seriousness.

"Lucy and I were taking a walk around the outer walkway, on the eastern side of the castle. Two men in guard uniforms approached us and asked her to come with them. I didn't recognize them. I got between them and Lucy. When I questioned them, they...they tossed me aside. The fall must have knocked me out, because I don't remember anything after that." She gave a hearty sniff, and her eyes filled with tears. "A guard—a *real* guard —found me. But Lucy was *gone*."

I nodded, putting the pieces together as she spoke. My heart clenched as I recognised the anguish in her face. It was my own pain, reflected back at me.

"Stavrok..." she said. Her slim hand found my arm. It was trembling. "I failed you. I couldn't keep her safe. I'm *so* sorry."

Her head dropped.

"No," I said. "This is not your fault, Cass. You couldn't have known."

"Will we get her back?" Cass wiped a tear from her face, listing to the side. She was still weak, clearly unable to stand unaided.

"We will," I replied. "I promise."

She gave me another weak smile and brought a hand up to her forehead, frowning when she saw blood. "Huh."

I turned to the guard on the other side of her.

"Take her to the infirmary and see to it that she gets immediate medical attention."

The guard snapped his heels and swept up Cass. She didn't protest, and her head lolled against his shoulder as he carried her off.

Assured that my cousin was being seen to, I turned back to the matter at hand.

Cass's state had distracted me from my initial spike of rage. Now my brain was cool and logical, drawing up plans, strategizing. I was in battle mode.

If Magnik wanted a war, he would get one.

I ASSEMBLED my chief advisors in the old map room in the center of the castle. The room had, at one time, been the scene of many war councils and state meetings, but there hadn't been a war waged in these lands since my grandfather's time. Consequently, it now lay quiet, the blinds drawn over the windows, slightly dingy from the years of abandonment.

With the help of Maddie and the others, I shook off the dust sheets and unfurled the maps that covered the walls, until the room was a flurry of activity.

Once everything was set up, I stood at the head of the table, looking out over the map of the country, laid out in miniature. I tried to imagine myself in my other form, flying low over the tiny hilltops and villages.

I glanced up, assessing all the expectant faces that sat around the table, waiting for me to speak. Maddie lingered in the corner of the room, her hands placed neatly behind her back. I nodded at her; grateful she had stayed.

In many ways, she was my only true ally in this room.

My hand dipped down, and I traced the carved, ridged hilltops that represented my ancestral lands. "Magnik has offered me a deal. If I give up these lands, he will guarantee Lucy's safe return."

The council absorbed my words. Looks of despair and anger passed over the heavily lined faces of the older men. They were my father's age, or older; old enough to know the stakes of Magnik's offer, and the value of the land beneath our feet.

They knew the magnitude of what lay ahead of us.

Slowly, but surely, I raised my head. I felt the weight of kingship settle across my shoulders, as heavy as it was on the day of my coronation.

"I'm not giving up *anything* to Magnik," I said, low and certain. "Not land, nor territory. And certainly not my queen."

"What are you going to do, sire?"

The question didn't come from any of the elders at the table.

It came from Maddie.

She gazed at me with hope and pride, like she could see something shining out of me that nobody else could.

"The only thing I can do. I'm going to launch an attack on Magnik's lands."

There was a rustle of movement around the table as the elders put their heads together and murmured to each other in low voices.

"Your Majesty, it has been over a century since any of the kingdoms have gone to war," Hillsen stated. "It would be... *could* be... catastrophic. For his people, and ours."

I bowed my head in acknowledgement, although frustration beat against the inside of my chest like a drum.

I was done with waiting around. I just wanted to get Lucy back, as soon as possible.

Even if I had to tear down every wall of Magnik's castle with my bare hands.

"Believe me, I am aware of the horrors that war will bring." I barely managed to keep the growl out of my voice. "But Magnik has left me with no choice. He struck first. He broke into my castle, hurt Cass, and stole away the woman I love."

The other council members looked grim, but I could see I was winning them over.

"My soulmate. You all know as well as I do, how long I've waited for her. I wish it hadn't come to this, but I won't rest until she's back where she belongs."

I knew in my heart I was right. There was no other choice.

I raised my chin, addressing the room. "Magnik must pay for what he has done."

EIGHTEEN

I don't know how, but I slept.

It was impossible to tell day from night in this place, and I didn't bother trying. I dozed on the thin wooden bench, imagining myself back in Stavrok's bed, surrounded by soft sheets and silk pillows.

Safe.

I jolted awake to the sound of heavy iron bars sliding free. The huge door swung open on its hinges for the first time since I'd arrived.

My chest tightened, and fear trickled down my spine.

A small, slight figure walked into the room. A woman, carrying a tray of food and a jug of water.

It would be impossible to mistake her for a servant. It wasn't just that her gown was a rich, deep blue color, and her hair elaborately decorated with crystal hairpins. There was something regal about her bearing. This woman was nobility.

She set down the tray on the bench beside me. I flinched, wondering if she might hurt me, and she quickly stepped back, her eyes wide and her expression sympathetic.

In fact, she looked about as nervous as I felt.

I gathered my wits, forcing myself to sit straight.

"Where am I?" I asked. "Where's Magnik? This *is* his dungeon, I presume."

Her eyes met mine and I was immediately drawn into her gaze. The irises were a startling shade of violet, and there almost seemed to be swirling mists in their depths, like there were hidden secrets in this woman that cried out to be explored.

I blinked a few times, dispelling the sense of mystery.

She smiled in a tentative manner, as if unsure of my response. "You're in Magnik's castle. Our castle," the woman said. Her voice was hesitant, apologetic.

Our castle?

"Who are you, his henchman?" I snapped. "No offense, but you're not exactly threatening."

That statement was only half-true. The woman was tiny—definitely a lot smaller than me—but those eyes hinted at an untold amount of power.

"I'm Marienne." Her voice was soft. She didn't seem perturbed by my sharp tone. "I'm King Magnik's wife."

Huh.

For some reason, I hadn't expected that. Magnik was a monster, and this woman—Marienne—did not fit with my idea of a monster's wife.

"Has he sent you here to get information?" I guessed. "Because I don't know *anything*. A few days ago, I didn't even know there were such things as dragons! And even if I did, I wouldn't tell you. You're wasting your time."

I crossed my arms, turning to face the wall.

"Magnik doesn't know I'm here." Marienne's voice was almost a whisper, and I detected a hint of fear in her tone.

I blinked. Despite myself, I inclined my head toward her, curious. "Seriously? Won't the guards tell him you stopped by?"

A wry smile ghosted across her face. "They didn't exactly notice me come in."

She held out her arm, and I watched as the air rippled around her fingers. Her outstretched limb grew fainter, fading until it became indistinguishable from the stone wall behind her.

"Whoa," I breathed, turning back properly to face her. "You're like a chameleon."

She laughed. The sound was light; it sparkled like silver bells. I thought how lovely it would be to hear such a sound on a regular basis, but instinct told me she didn't laugh often. "Let's just say I'm the master of hide and seek," she said.

No shit.

"Are you a witch?"

"The correct term is a sorceress." She fiddled with the ends of her hair. "Some of us are born with unusual abilities. My powers were the reason Magnik took me for his bride."

She looked downcast, and I didn't blame her. I couldn't imagine being married to someone like Magnik.

I felt a flash of pity for Marienne. Clearly, King Magnik was not the man of her dreams.

Still, what do I know?

"Aren't you his..." I fumbled. "Soulmate, or what-have-you?"

She flushed. "No. Not every monarch accepts his soulmate." Her voice dropped again into a whisper, even though we were completely alone. "Magnik bought me from my family because he craves power above all else. Total dominion, over his people and all the other kingdoms. To him, I am an instrument—I can give him these things, if I choose to."

"Do you want to?"

As soon as the question left my lips, I knew the answer. This was not an evil queen standing in front of me. Marienne was a victim, just as much as I currently was, sitting imprisoned in this dungeon.

She sighed, a deep, fractured sound that tore out of the very depths of her body.

"No." Crystalline tears welled up in those otherworldly eyes, making them almost luminescent. She blinked them back as if determined not to lose control of her emotions. "When I was a child, I hoped to be... more. I dreamed of marrying a man who loved me for *me*, not for my magic. I have never wanted to hurt anyone. The things Magnik wants, the things he has planned... they are wrong. I never wanted any of this. My parents sold me to him and forced me to be his queen."

She wiped her cheeks and shook her head fiercely.

My mind drifted back to my argument with Stavrok.

It could have only been a few hours ago, but it felt like a distant memory. I frowned. "I think I know how you feel. Kind of. I'm not really here by choice, either. This is all brand new to me. Stavrok just found me and carried me off." I snorted. "He's not exactly an expert on the human world. God only knows how he found me."

Marienne didn't reply. Instead, she bit her bottom lip.

I tilted my head. "What?"

"I showed him the way to you." She glanced away from me. "He... he was hurting, Lucy. He has been alone for years, waiting for his soulmate. I offered to help him look, and my vision led him straight to you."

Shock ran through me. Destiny, fate... these weren't things I'd held much faith in before. Maybe I'd been wrong to judge them so harshly.

"Are you telling me that it's true?" I croaked. "I *am* Stavrok's soulmate?"

She gave me a puzzled frown. "Yes, of course. I'm surprised you even have to ask. The fates have crafted you for each other. You're a perfect match."

I thought about fate. I pictured a golden thread, weaving

through my life, connecting me to everyone I met. Stavrok, Cass…
and now Marienne, seeing me in her vision, and us meeting again
like this.

Marienne reached out a hand toward me, then dropped it
again. Sadness filled her expression. "If my actions have caused
you any pain, I am truly sorry, Lucy."

"It's not your fault," I said quickly, automatically, before I realized it was true. "You were trying to help."

"I was." She held out a hand again, palm upwards. "May I?"

When I nodded, I felt something pass over me, like a shadow.

"Is that your magic, Marienne?"

"It is. Don't be afraid."

I smiled at her. "I'm not." Her magic was feather-light and soft
to the touch. It felt… comforting, more than anything.

Still, I hesitated before finally placing my palm in hers. Her
eyes slid closed, and she was silent for a long moment.

I felt her going through my mind, turning over the chapters of
my life like they were pages in a book. There were glimpses of my
childhood, the house I grew up in, the children I had cared for.

There were one or two doors that I didn't want her to open. I
turned her away, sharp, before she could peek into *those*.

Nope. Stay out!

She huffed a laugh, startled, and dropped my hand. When she
opened her eyes and met my gaze, she grinned.

"You have a little natural magical ability yourself, Lucy. You
protected your secrets from me without even thinking about it."

I had magic? If I thought about *that* for too long, my head
would explode. "What did you find out? Anything interesting?"

Her eyebrows drew together. "Oh yes." She moved forward, as
if to provide a hug, then clearly thought better of it. Instead, she
gently patted my arm. "Lucy, you're pregnant."

I went cold. "What?"

She didn't say anything else. She didn't have to. As much as I wanted to protest, I knew, somewhere deep in my core, that she was right.

I had known for a while. I just hadn't been able to accept it. It was way too soon for any symptoms, and Stavrok and I had only slept together twice...

I groaned. *Stavrok.*

This was what he'd wanted, all along.

To my surprise, I felt a pang of *something* when I thought about him.

I miss him.

This was all wrong. We should have found out this information together. I would have broken the news quietly, in bed, or over the breakfast table. It would have been our little secret, a private joy we could have shared before we told the rest of the kingdom.

But he was God-only-knew where, and I was here.

Oh, shit.

"You realize that, once Magnik discovers your pregnancy, your value to him will only increase," Marienne said. She looked as panicked as I felt. "An unwed soulmate is one thing, but the mother of Stavrok's heir? That's quite another."

I grabbed at her hand, still resting on my arm, and clasped it tightly.

"Please, I'm begging you. I know I'm asking for a lot here. And I know you have no reason to do me any favors, but from one woman to another." I took a deep, shaky gulp of air. "Please don't tell him."

"Of course, I won't." Her gaze was solemn. "I won't speak of it, Lucy. I promise."

I let out a breath I didn't even know I'd beenholding, and released her hand. "Thank you, Marienne."

"Call me Mari, please." She glanced at the door, as if she was worried her husband might burst in at any moment. "I'll do my best to protect you. But, aside from my magic, I have no real power here."

I thought about Stavrok. His strength, his fury. The way he looked at me, like he would do anything to keep me safe.

I thought about the child or children that I carried inside me. His children.

"I appreciate your kindness, Mari." I hoped her magic, along with my soulmate bond with Stavrok, would be enough to protect me and the baby. "Stavrok will be here soon to rescue me, and then all will be well once again."

I had to believe that, because the alternative was not an option.

NINETEEN

STAVROK

In my dragon form, I glided through the air, zeroing in on my destination. There was no time to waste. Messages delivered to the other kingdoms had ensured that they would stay far away from this fight.

They had agreed, some more warily than others, but it wasn't their feud. My own guards were on standby and would head this way the moment I sent the signal. But I hoped I wouldn't have to.

This was personal. Between Magnik and me.

The peace that had protected us all for so long now hung in the balance, fragile as a gossamer thread. It was my duty to settle this. The lives of my people, of our whole world, hung in the balance.

Magnik's castle sat lower than mine. It was nestled into the black mountainside like a forbidden secret. It was small, as far as dragon castles went.

The front of the structure hid an elaborate sprawl of tunnels and caves that wound deep within the mountain, making it almost impossible to attack through traditional means.

The castle itself was just a façade, a deception. Just like Magnik himself.

I let the air currents carry me closer, barely moving my wings. I hoped the cloud cover would serve to conceal my approach, but I knew that every eye in that castle would be trained toward the sky.

Magnik would be waiting for me.

Well, I was coming for him.

My hackles were up. Why bother hiding anymore?

I let out a roar of displeasure that echoed around the rocky hilltops. A tongue of scalding flame shot from my mouth and illuminated the heavens like a lightning bolt.

If they didn't know I was here before, they certainly did now.

I wasn't some common thief, creeping into enemy territory under the cover of darkness. I was King Stavrok of Bravdok, son of Tyton and Eris.

I was coming to take back what had been stolen from me. Fire would rain down from the sky on whoever got in my way.

I swept into a low dive. My wings stretched wide, cutting through the air with ease. I cast a dark shadow over the ground as I flew.

I sent a silent prayer out into the swirling storm, hoping against hope that Lucy might somehow hear me.

Wherever you are, love, I'm coming for you.

I let out another billowing fireball, sweeping in a wide arc as I neared the castle's main watchtower.

Tiny figures stood on the parapets, aiming large crossbows into the sky.

Directly at me.

I roared, and my wings arched backwards.

I was close enough to watch as their eyes widened with fear.

They loosed their arrows, striking against my chest, snagging against my wings.

In human form, they would have killed me a hundred times over.

As a dragon? The arrows were as harmless as flies.

I shook myself, dislodging the arrows from my leathery wings. The thick scales that protected my chest smoothed back into place, and I continued my advance, unperturbed.

It would take far more than ordinary crossbow bolts to slow me down.

I was more than a dragon shifter. The blood that ran through my veins was the blood of a king. I was stronger than most others of my kind, and much harder to kill.

One of the archers dropped his weapon, fleeing from his post. The other cowered in the corner as I lit up the stone wall.

I barely spared him a glance. He wasn't my concern, after all.

I couldn't enter the castle in my dragon form. I was too large, too cumbersome. So, I landed on the wall and with difficulty, quieted the seething fire of rage in the pit of my stomach. I felt myself shrink down, my limbs reforming themselves, my vision changing.

Once in human form, I grabbed the abandoned crossbow and pointed it at the terrified archer.

"Where is she?" I snapped.

The archer pointed one trembling finger toward a low doorway set into the wall of the tower.

"That way, sire."

I ignored the numbness that settled through my bare limbs with the cold air and shouldered my crossbow. I half-turned in the direction he indicated before a thought occurred to me.

I was storming into the heart of enemy territory. It might be better if I weren't naked into the bargain.

"Let's make a trade," I said. "Your life for your trousers."

The archer didn't need to be told twice.

After I dressed, I strode through the castle doors, into the unknown.

~

Magnik's castle was chillier than the one I called home.

The walls were bare and dark. The only light came from the torches that burned at intervals in ornate iron cages.

I shivered.

Moving quietly, keeping my head low and my senses on high alert, I couldn't help but feel uneasy.

It had all been too simple. The lack of defenses, the empty hallway.

It was as if Magnik wanted me here.

Like I was playing right into his hands.

I shook off the prickle on the back of my neck and kept moving. I had no choice, after all.

I have to find Lucy.

Through my carelessness, I had broken the one promise I had sworn to her I would uphold. I had allowed her to fall into danger.

A cluster of voices emanated from the end of the corridor.

Finally.

As stealthily as possible, I slid the crossbow into position.

I would have preferred the familiar weight of a sword in my hands, but I was nothing if not adaptable.

It struck me again how impulsive I was being. My plan of attack was hasty, instinctive, fuelled by nothing more than the drive to rescue my mate.

Which, of course, was exactly what Magnik had anticipated.

My fingers tightened around the crossbow as I rounded the corner.

I took the guards by surprise. The nearest one didn't have time to draw his sword before I kicked him squarely in the chest and sent him flying into the opposite wall.

I whirled around, bringing the barrel of the crossbow up hard against the sword that swung down on me. I grunted with the force of the blow and twisted, lodging the sword in place and sending its owner staggering backwards without his weapon.

The third had taken advantage of my distraction; I hissed as the edge of a blade slashed into my arm.

I slid sideways. His sword cut through air and he staggered, off balance.

I pulled the sword free from the crossbow and turned it in my palm, testing the heft. Adrenaline coursed through me.

I may be far from home, in mortal danger, but I was in my element here.

And now I was properly armed.

The clang of metal against metal echoed off the stone walls as I faced down the two guards.

Their companion lay motionless on the ground, stunned by the force of my blow.

Even though the fight was two against one, I sensed my opponents growing tired. Their movements were clumsy, and I pressed my advantage, driving them further and further down the corridor.

Was this the first real fight they'd ever been in?

I wheeled around and slammed the hilt of my sword against the head of one of the men. He went down easily.

The last of the men fought with more determination than his friends, his face twisted into an ugly sneer.

A new thought occurred to me.

These men could have been the ones to infiltrate my castle. The ones who hurt Cass, the ones who snatched Lucy away...

I let out an inhuman snarl and pushed forward.

He staggered back, and I twisted my blade upwards, sending his weapon flying to the ground with a clatter.

I pressed the edge of my sword up against his neck, a savage thrill running through me at the way his eyes widened.

"Enough of this," I said. "Where is she?"

"The throne room."

I pushed the blade higher and watched his face grow paler.

"Ah! Please, it is no trick, Your Majesty. The king has your mate close by him, at the heart of the palace."

I narrowed my eyes. My mind raced; through vague memories of state dinners I had attended as a child, I knew that the throne room had to be somewhere nearby.

I moved as if to sheath my sword, and he scuttled away from me. I swung a glancing blow into the side of his head, and he slumped over, unconscious.

As I prowled through the castle, I stuck close to the shadows, pressing myself into alcoves and crevices as I neared my destination.

The voices ahead were growing louder. The corridor widened out, intricate marble stonework beneath my bare feet.

Magnik's family line was as ancient as my own. It pained me that he had thrown his noble heritage into the dirt by what he had done.

Outside the wide double doors leading to the throne room, I halted. Beyond the doors was only silence.

I pressed my hand against the handle. I could hear nothing but low murmuring from the other side of the doors. I had the element of surprise, but that would only last for a few seconds. I had to make that time count.

So far, the guards had been easy enough to handle.

Too easy...

I couldn't shake the sense that the battle hadn't yet started.

Whatever faced me on the other side of these doors, was when the real fight would begin.

If he's harmed her in any way, I'll kill him where he stands.

With a huff, I shouldered through the entranceway, and entered the cavernous throne room.

It was just as vast as I remembered. The walls stretched so high that the ceiling was barely visible. Black polished marble cast dark reflections underfoot, and the sparse décor was ornate, cold, and uncomfortable.

A raised platform held two thrones that were framed by carved columns.

Queen Marienne sat on one of the thrones, but she no longer looked like herself. One of her eyes was swollen shut, and that whole side of her face was black and purple with bruising. Instead of sitting straight and regal, she hunched over to one side. She barely seemed strong enough to hold herself upright at all.

Had Magnik beaten her? Was this new or something she'd endured from him many times? Pity filled me for the queen, but I had no time to dwell on that.

My gaze swept across the other throne, which was empty, and landed on Magnik. He stood in the center of the platform in front of another figure, his bulk hiding the person from my view. I could see the person had been tied to one of the dark columns rising up from the platform.

As Magnik bent close to his prisoner, I spotted a familiar head of blonde hair, and my pulse began to race. The bastard had Lucy in restraints.

He will pay dearly for this.

His back straightened, and slowly he turned. He must have sensed my presence.

"Stavrok." Magnik's voice echoed through the empty space with a note of satisfaction, and my skin prickled. "We were wondering when you would show up. I was beginning to worry you weren't coming."

Behind him, Lucy's eyes widened at the sight of me.

White cloth had been tied over her mouth, and my icy rage mounted.

There was nothing Magnik could do to contain her temper, though. It was plain to see, even from this distance. Lucy's eyes were bright and wild, and her cheeks were flushed with fury. She didn't wear the whole damsel-in-distress thing well. Perhaps they had expected a human to remain silent and compliant.

I could have told them otherwise. She twisted and turned against restraints that would never budge, but she didn't give up.

Pride sparked in my chest.

She wasn't one to go down without a fight, apparently. She may have been a human, surrounded by shapeshifters more powerful than she would ever be, but the courage in her eyes made my heart skip.

We were more alike than she knew.

"These are the actions of a coward, not a king," I snarled, turning my attention to Magnik. "Lucy has no part in this. Let her go."

Magnik spread his hands wide, moving away from her and descending the steps of the platform with unhurried ease.

"I gave you my terms, Stavrok. It's a fair trade. I get my lands, you get your mate back, safe and sound. Everyone's happy."

I fought the rage that simmered inside me, threatening to spill out and consume them all.

Up on the platform, a small movement caught my eye. Marienne?

She had slumped further in her seat, as if about to topple to the floor. But her gaze was fixed on me. I almost heard her voice in my head. *Hold onto your rage. Use it. But don't lose control.*

I blinked, and turned back to Magnik as he spoke.

"I have been waiting for this a long time, Stavrok. You've grown too comfortable, content to squander your riches. They lie buried in the earth, crumbling away."

I gave a growl. "My duty is to protect my own."

My gaze darted to Lucy. She had grown still in her confines; clearly, she was hanging on every word.

"Meanwhile," I said, "you hide away in your inner sanctum and let your men fight on your behalf! You're not fit to hold this kingdom."

"I tried to reason with you." Magnik strode close, his face twisting into an ugly scowl. "Year after year, I offered you trade agreements, business deals. You wouldn't take anything I offered you! So, now I have taken something of *yours.*"

He swept out a hand, indicating Lucy.

I said nothing. Anger rooted me to the spot. I focused on drawing long, measured breaths, in and out. *Don't lose control.*

But if he touches her...

I would tear down every wall in this godforsaken place and burn the lot. The hot fire of rage flooded through me, startling in its intensity. It burned brighter, building and building, until I could barely see the man standing in front of me.

"You've left me no choice, Stavrok." Magnik inclined his head, regarding me with narrowed eyes.

When I opened my mouth, it was the dragon within me who framed the words on my lips.

"Neither have you. King Magnik, I challenge you in combat. No armies to protect you. No more of your men will fall at my hand." I straightened and swung my sword in a circle through the air, the metal blade flashing in the flickering torchlight. "Just you against me."

Magnik's expression flickered as he absorbed my words.

I held firm. My gaze was sure and steady, but already I could feel adrenaline thrumming through my veins.

I spared a thought for my parents. I knew in the depths of my heart that it was *their* legacy I was protecting. For the first time since I took the throne, I saw the path ahead of me with perfect clarity.

And Lucy...

I had put her in grave peril.

She had been right, all along. I had been too blind and selfish to see it before. This wasn't her world, and she would never be safe here. It had been madness to ask her to stay.

I couldn't dwell on my pending heartbreak. I had to focus on the task at hand.

For the first time in a hundred years, a dragon king in this land of Fire and Ice had drawn his sword against another.

Magnik stepped forward. His eyes were steely, and when he spoke his voice was cold.

"Very well. I accept your challenge."

TWENTY

I continued to struggle against the bonds that held me tight against the marble column, listing every curse I knew until they became a soothing, rhythmic chant in the back of my mind.

Fighting the bindings was pointless, but I couldn't just wait here and do nothing while Stavrok threw himself into this fight.

This wasn't some courtyard sparring match. There was an odd glitter in Magnik's eye, and something about the way he tilted his head as he and Stavrok circled each other made my blood run cold.

Nobody had to tell me; I knew the truth.

He won't stop fighting. Not until Stavrok is dead.

A flash of terror passed through me when I pictured Stavrok's lifeless body lying on the marble floor.

I feared for my own life too, held at the mercy of such a tyrant. But that fear was soon eclipsed by the realization that had been haunting me ever since I'd found out I held Stavrok's heirs inside me.

If I were to live, I would surely be kept as a prisoner here. And, sooner or later, I would begin to show...

Magnik will never allow Stavrok's bloodline to survive.

I narrowed my eyes and focused on drawing deep, cleansing breaths. From my position, I had a clear view of both kings as they circled each other, swords drawn.

This is insane. This is totally insane...

I chanced a glance at Marienne, whose throne lay a few feet to my left. I could only see the outline of her profile, but she was hunched over and from the looks of her, badly hurt.

What had that bastard done to her? Had he caught her visiting me in the dungeon? Delivering food, and a hint of kindness?

I wished I could somehow communicate with her. I was certain that she didn't support her husband's plan to kill Stavrok.

More than that, I knew, deep down, that she was just as afraid of him as I was.

At the sound of metal crashing against metal, my gaze snapped back to the duel at the center of the throne room.

The two men had moved closer to the platform, allowing me to get a good look at Stavrok. His chest glistened with effort as he drove Magnik back into the far corner, sword swinging through the air. There was a fresh cut on his arm, and he was grunting with exertion.

His words from earlier came back to me.

No more of your men will fall at my hand.

It seemed that Magnik had taken the coward's route, hiding in the shadows while his guardsmen took on Stavrok.

He's exhausted already.

Despite his injuries, Stavrok was clearly the better fighter. He stayed on the attack, forcing Magnik to parry a volley of savage blows in quick succession.

Frustrated, I bit down on the cloth that gagged me and craned my neck back, trying to work the material free against the column.

I was powerless to help, but if I was going to die, I didn't want to be without my voice.

I wouldn't give Magnik the satisfaction of killing me in silence.

I huffed with the effort of my task, and my heart thrummed in my chest when someone gave a loud shout of pain and fury.

The harsh panting of the two kings filled the hall.

Magnik toppled to his knees like a puppet whose strings had been cut. His sword clattered to the floor beside him; he clutched his right arm against his body, holding it while dark crimson seeped through his sleeve.

Stavrok staggered backwards. He kicked the sword away from Magnik and wiped a hand over his mouth.

Over Magnik's kneeling form, he caught my gaze.

Up until this moment, the dragon warrior was all I had seen. He was the one who had come to rescue me. Aggressive, domineering, driven by fury and power, the beast lit him up from within with unearthly force.

But for a single heart-wrenching moment, all I could see was the man beneath. Stavrok.

He held the sword high, poised to strike in cold blood. One blow, that was all it would take. His eyes were wide, filled with adrenaline and something else I couldn't decipher.

Those icy blue eyes, that only a few days ago had been so mysterious.

They pierced through me, and I froze to the spot. Stavrok seemed unsure, watching my face like he was transfixed.

Magnik reached for something strapped to his calf, and I caught the flash of a silver dagger as he slid it into his hand.

With a sharp jerk of my head, the cloth tied around my mouth loosened, and I managed to shimmy it down to my neck.

Magnik, still on his knees, lunged forward like a snake.

I screamed, "Look out!"

Stavrok whirled backwards. The dagger sliced through thin air, half a second too late.

Magnik hissed with anger.

"A cheap trick," Stavrok spat. "I should have known you would resort to low tactics, Magnik. You won't fool me again."

Magnik scrambled to his feet. He sliced upwards with the dagger, twisting the hilt of Stavrok's blade with his own.

"You gave me the chance to strike. You had the chance to kill me, but you didn't." His face twisted, and a taunting smile slid across his face. "You're weak. *Soft*. Just like your parents. What exactly happened to them, again?"

Stavrok gave a snarl and his attack intensified, the speed of his thrusts increasing. Magnik stumbled a little against the brute force of his onslaught. Both men were struggling to gain the upper hand. The air felt thick and heavy; it crackled with tension. I wanted to scream out again, do something to help, but I didn't want to distract Stavrok.

"How dare you?" Stavrok roared. His eyes were molten. I could feel his rage even from this distance; it burned like a brazier. "You're not worthy to hold this kingdom. You are no king!"

"Stand aside, Stavrok." Magnik's face split into a leering grin. His skin was pale and clammy from the fight, and his hair fell lankly across his face. I shuddered as his eyes darted to me momentarily. "I'll let you live. You can go free, walk out the door and find a new life, far from here. I'm sure there are other maidens who would have you. *Worthy* ones. Dragon-born, proud and strong."

His grin shifted until he was baring his teeth.

"I'll keep the human. She will bring me some amusement." His eyes crept over me again, taking in my body, lingering in a way that made my skin crawl. "For a night or two, at least."

Stavrok swung at Magnik's weapon, grunting with the effort. Repeatedly, he beat down on the arrogant king. There was a heat in the room, a fire in his eyes. His dragon was close to the surface. I could feel it.

Magnik's silver dagger was dislodged from his hand and went flying through the air, landing with a *clink* against the marble floor. I stared, amazed, as it came to rest just below my feet.

Then, with a final, earth-shaking growl, Stavrok raised his sword and drove it through Magnik's heart.

~

Stavrok

THE MOMENT MAGNIK'S body hit the floor, Marienne stumbled off her throne. She didn't look grief-stricken, but *amazed*, like she couldn't quite believe what had just happened.

I raised my sword again, turning to face her, but the gesture was half-hearted.

The truth was, I had no idea what she was capable of or if she was truly friend or foe.

For all I knew, she was about to kill me right now, with nothing more than a magical incantation or a flicker of her fingers.

Slowly, her hands came up. She held them out in front of her in a gesture of peace, her one good eye fixed on me, her face drawn.

"Stavrok… please. This wasn't my doing." Her good eye swirled with color, blue mingling with deep purple and almost matching the bruises on her face. "You have to believe me. I never wanted any part of this. My husband—"

"Was an evil man." I found my voice at last.

Magnik's body lay between us where he'd fallen. Around him, scorch marks were burned into the marble, forming a crater.

The death of a dragon king was a rare event indeed. The marks proved what I already knew: his fire had gone out for good.

"He was. Truly, an evil man. One who has kept me as a slave and a prisoner for years." Marienne inclined her head. "Thank you for freeing me. At last. Your mate, she—"

"Would quite like to be untied now, thank you very much," Lucy called out.

My gaze snapped to Lucy, who was struggling against her restraints. I hurried over to her and broke the ties one by one.

She stretched, rotating her shoulders and groaning. "God, of course you can break them with your *bare hands*, Stavrok."

She rolled her eyes, and my heart swelled.

"Lucy," I said simply.

I reached out. I wanted to pull her close to me, kiss her deeply. We had been separated for what felt like an eternity. Her mere presence was intoxicating. I closed my eyes, steadying myself against the pulse of want that surged through me.

I'd never believed people when they'd said my father died of a broken heart the day my mother died. It didn't seem possible that a man as strong as he, could die so easily, so quickly.

But today, for the first time, I realized that I would not want to live without Lucy. And if such a love grew through the years, then I finally understood how my father could give up on life once his mate died.

I settled for running my hands over her arms, and then cupping her face. "Are you hurt? Did he—"

"Hey, hey!" Her hands found mine, and she wound our fingers together. "Stavrok, I'm fine. I'm absolutely fine. You, on the other hand, are *hurt*."

I spared a glance down at the deep gash that cut into my shoulder. "Never mind that now."

She shook her head at me.

"I thought you worked in a day-care center, not a hospital." I sighed, allowing her to take my arm and wrap the cloth gag around the wound, securing it over my shoulder.

She frowned at the makeshift bandage, smoothing it several times before stepping back, satisfied. "I can play nurse with the best of them."

My eyes searched her face for a heated moment.

"I bet you can."

Somewhere behind us, Marienne coughed.

Right. There's unfinished business to attend to, here.

I placed a hand on Lucy's shoulder and turned to regard the sorceress.

She wrapped her arms around her middle and glanced at Magnik, whose remains lay at her feet.

"What happens now?" Her eyes dipped, and her voice filled with regret. "I can't tell you how sorry I am for all this."

I struggled with my warring impulses. On the one hand, this woman was a sorceress and possibly dangerous. Whether or not it was on purpose, she had started the chain of events that led to Lucy's capture and imprisonment.

On the other hand... I closed my eyes.

If it hadn't been for her, I never would have known Lucy existed.

"Stavrok..." Lucy laid a hand on my arm, and I turned into her body like a sapling toward the sun. "She helped me. She protected me from Magnik, as much as she could. And look what he did to her in return. I believe her."

I nodded. I couldn't understand what Marienne had gone through living with Magnik for the last ten years, but if she'd helped Lucy in her hour of need, then the sorceress had earned my mercy.

"Very well." I surveyed Marienne, the once beautiful queen,

who appeared right now to be broken. "There remains the small matter of choosing a new king. You have no heirs, my lady."

There was no way of putting it delicately. Magnik's bloodline stopped with him.

Some might call that a mercy.

"No," Marienne said. "Magic has given me many things, but no child."

As though to prove her point, she lifted her hands and magic began to swirl around her face and torso.

She straightened up, and her face began to heal right in front of our eyes. The bruising disappeared first, then her eye opened, and finally she was her usual self again.

"If you could do that by yourself, why didn't you do it before?" Lucy demanded, reaching out to touch Marienne's freshly healed face.

A tremble of a smile lifted Marienne's lips. "He told me after the beating that if I took away any of my own pain and suffering, he would do the same to you, Lucy. Or worse." She shuddered. "He was very cruel."

Fresh anger rolled through me at her words. "He was no king." I growled, wishing I could kill the bastard again.

"Marienne, you know that only one of royal blood may anoint a dragon king," I said, primarily for Lucy's benefit. I could tell that she was listening closely to every word. "I will be in touch. We must find a new king for these lands. One worthy of the name, this time."

Marienne's eyes flickered. She bit her lip, her brows drawing together.

"What is it?" I asked.

"There was a boy. An illegitimate half-brother. Magnik told me of him, and a few years ago I secretly sought him out. He lives in the village." Her voice grew soft, dropping to a whisper, even though Lucy and I were the only people in the room. "His mother was sent away by Magnik's father when she was pregnant. I don't know much beyond that."

I processed the information and gave a final nod to her. She returned the nod, watching me with careful eyes.

Lucy murmured a farewell as we swept out of the throne room. Their eyes met with a friendliness that made me wonder what had passed between them while Lucy had been a prisoner here.

"Let's get out of here," I said, sliding my arm around her waist and squeezing. I craved her warmth, her proximity. "Time to return home."

"I don't know where the front entrance is." Lucy looked from left to right as we found ourselves at the end of a corridor. "I didn't exactly get the grand tour, I'm afraid."

I hoped that one day we would return to this castle as honored guests. I wanted to show Lucy that my world wasn't all darkness and bloodlust. There was laughter to be found here too, and friendship.

If all goes to plan, we shall be back.

"We're not leaving by the front door," I said, drawing away from her to pull open the door that led out onto a narrow rooftop.

"We're not?" Lucy wrapped her arms around herself, shivering from the rush of cold air. She had to shout to be heard over the howling wind. "Then how are... *oh.*"

I strode a few paces away from her and shook out my limbs. Deep within my chest, the dragon unfurled its wings. It was ready to go, fired from the fight and the joy of reuniting with Lucy.

My claws emerged. My scales rippled, smooth and dark, and my wings beat the air, making the snowdrifts swirl. Lucy tipped back her head and laughed, and in my mind's eye I saw the night we met.

The first time she had seen my dragon.

We had been strangers to each other, then. She had been nothing but terrified.

Now, there was a warmth in her face. Genuine affection in her eyes.

I didn't allow myself to believe it could be anything more than that.

If you really love her, you will let her go.

Without prompting, she clambered onto my back, throwing her arms around my neck, apparently having forgotten all about the cold.

Together, we took off into the snow-filled sky.

CHAPTER

TWENTY-ONE

LUCY

After our exhilarating ride home, Stavrok swept me into the entrance hall, cradled in his arms, and demanded a warm cloak, which was duly provided. The heavy garment lay across my shoulders as I sat on a large chair in the hallway.

Stavrok paced up and down the marble floors. It was unsettling to watch, to say the least.

His eyes flashed, and he kept glancing back at me, over and over, like he was certain I would disappear right in front of him.

I wanted him to stop pacing the hallway. It was making me nervous. The longer the silence stretched out, the less I certain I became.

There was so much I wanted to say, but for the first time, I wasn't sure where we stood.

He had been all fire and rage from the moment he'd stepped into the throne room, but his behavior toward me had been different, even once he'd defeated Magnik.

I couldn't shake the feeling that he was holding me at arm's length, somehow.

He's just killed a rival king, and you're wondering why he hasn't taken you to bed already? Jeez, Lucy.

My face heated, and I went back to flicking stray snowflakes from my hair.

As much as the pacing annoyed me, I felt sure that it was the only thing keeping him from shifting into his dragon form and wreaking havoc.

"You could have been hurt, Lucy," he burst out, dragging his hands over his face.

I gaped, at a loss. I had never seen him like this. The stoicism that I'd come to expect from him had vanished. He looked terrified.

"You could have been killed," he said, "and it would have been my fault."

I reached out and put a hand on his arm. The motion stilled him. I pitched my voice so that it came out soft and soothing.

"I'm fine, Stavrok." I cupped his cheek and turned his face, looking deep into those mesmerizing eyes. "Look at me. You saved me."

After the darkness of Magnik's realm, this castle felt somehow lighter and airier than before. The light shafted through the windows, shading Stavrok's face with gold. I felt warmed just by being near him.

Stavrok shook his head even as he drew me closer. He slid one hand up my back, burying it in my hair.

"I'd rather be apart from you, if it would keep you safe," he murmured, dropping a kiss onto my forehead. "The human world carries far less dangers. It would better for you to return there, and be safe, than to stay here and risk your life in such a way again."

I gasped at his rejection. He wanted me to go home? No!

"You want me to leave?" I whispered, struggling to say the words through the pain of my heart breaking in my chest.

There was nothing for me back there. My future lay right here.

"Of course not." His voice rumbled through my chest, and I leaned into his solid frame with a sigh. "It would be the greatest pain imaginable to let you out of my sight. But I know now how much you mean to me. How precious you are. I can't risk you like that again, Lucy."

My heart skipped.

"Oh," was all I managed to say.

He's willing to let me go back.

I should be happy.

Why aren't I?

A couple of days ago, the prospect of freedom would have filled me with joy. Now, all I felt was a sharp ache at the thought of leaving this place.

"I'm so sorry for all the distress that I've caused you, my love." He stroked my cheek, cupping my chin with his broad hand. "More than I can say."

I clasped his hand with both of mine and brought it up to my mouth, pressing a kiss to his palm. His eyes widened, but he didn't pull away.

"I'm not." My voice was bold and steady. Suddenly, I knew exactly what I wanted to say. "Once upon a time, I would've chosen the safer option. But I had a lot of time to think when I was locked up in that dungeon."

I took a deep, shuddering breath. "Being here has made me realize what love is, Stavrok. What loyalty is. I don't want to stay because some magic vision says so. I want to stay because we belong together. My life is here, now. I belong by your side, as your queen."

"You... *want* to stay?"

"I do."

He eyed me for several heart-stopping moments, before his

face broke into the sunniest grin I had ever seen. I grinned back, buoyed up by his joy.

"In the castle? In this land?"

"Yes!"

Before I knew what was happening, he had me in a tight bearhug. My feet lifted off the floor, and I giggled, pressing my face into his chest.

"It's probably for the best that I stay here, anyway," I added when he set me down. My grin softened into a loving smile, and I pressed a hand to my belly.

His gaze turned quizzical.

"I don't think human doctors know that much about shapeshifter babies," I said.

He looked at me, stunned, before he let out a sharp, delighted burst of laughter. "You're..."

"I am." I grabbed one of his hands, putting it on my stomach.

There was nothing to feel, not yet, but the warmth of his hand felt good against my skin. I imagined the sensations that would follow in the coming months; the tiny, growing life I held inside of me.

When he finally spoke, his voice was soft and wondering. "You are incredible."

"I know," I replied cheekily. "You're not so bad yourself."

"I suppose I have no choice but to keep you by my side now." He swept me in, kissing me hard until we both pulled back, breathless.

"How terrible for me," I said, running my hands over his arms and giggling. "However shall I cope?"

Stavrok's gaze turned serious. "Come with me."

Not like I had a choice, but I held tight to his neck as he swept me up into his arms and charged down the hall and into his bedroom.

He placed me on the bed and went straight for the dresser near the door. He opened a drawer, took something out, then turned to me with a bashful smile.

He came straight back and reached out for my hand.

"Lucy." He knelt gracefully in front of me.

My heart started hammering. If I hadn't already been flushed from his kiss, I was certain I would be glowing red.

"I have to ask. Officially, that is. Will you stay here, with me? Will you be my queen, now and always?"

"What about Daphne?" I whispered. He'd said she lied, but the pain of that moment still sat badly within me.

He growled. "How would you like her punished for lying to you so maliciously?"

I swallowed hard. I didn't want her punished... I wanted her, gone. "Um. Can we move her? I don't really want her in the castle anymore."

He nodded. "Done. She will be reassigned to a job at the other end of the village. You will never see her in our home, again."

I took a breath and let it out slowly. That was better.

I smiled this time. "Then... my answer is," I put my hands on either side of his face, drawing him up until his lips met mine. "I will. Of course."

His eyes glowed adoringly before they heated, darkened. He straightened fully before hitching me up like I weighed nothing at all.

I squealed.

Damn, I'm never going to get used to that.

I laughed freely as I wrapped my legs around his waist, uncaring of the fact that the door to the hallway was still open.

I had missed him. I *wanted* him.

I whispered a formless, breathy plea into his ear, and he pressed his hot mouth into my neck, growling when I gave a full body shudder. I could feel his hardness pressing into my core. Soon, there would be nothing between us. I wanted to feel all of him against me. Every inch of his powerful form.

My king, I thought, before he lay me down on the bed.

All mine.

EPILOGUE

STAVROK

"We're going to be late," I called through the open door of our bedchamber. "I can make excuses if you would rather stay, my love."

Lucy bobbed up into the doorway, face flushed with exertion. My impatience melted away at the sight of my beautiful wife, and I swept into the room behind her, wrapping my arms around her shoulders.

"Help me with my dress?" She looked over her shoulder, and I obliged, buttoning each of the tiny buttons from her waist to her neckline. Some maid or other would surely have to struggle with *those* later.

I peered over her shoulder at the finely carved trio of cribs that clustered around the wide, arched window, positioned to catch the best of the sunlight.

Or rather, I peered at what lay inside them.

Our babies nestled in their soft blankets. The girls, Jessa and Vanya, were fast asleep.

My son, Anselm, blinked up at me. His sleepy eyes were

fringed with soft, downy lashes. They were wide, and the same guileless shade of blue as his mother's.

I leaned down to press a kiss onto the fluffy head of hair before drawing away reluctantly, smiling when he gave a gurgle.

Our brood was strong and healthy. Human and dragon blood flowed through their veins, and they were no weaker for it.

They had the fair coloring of their mother, but already they had a glimmer in their eyes, that tell-tale spark of light.

A light that told me, one day, they would be powerful shapeshifters.

I chanced a glance back at them before I drew my arm around my wife's waist and escorted her out of the room.

"They're in good hands," Lucy murmured, leaning up to press a palm against my cheek. I grimaced at the fact she could read me so easily, and she laughed. "Maddie will be with them the whole time!"

"I know, I know," I said, tugging at the formal collar of my jacket a little as we descended the wide central staircase. "I'm not worried."

She leveled me with a smirk. I could read the disbelief in her eyes.

"I'm picturing your dragon curled up around them like nest eggs," she joked. "Or a pile of golden treasure."

She had told me about some of the legends of our kind, fanciful stories that humans had been passing down to each other for generations. They amused me on the cold winter nights, when Lucy and I would sit beside a roaring fire and talk into the small hours.

"They *are* my treasures," I replied, simple and honest. "As are you, my Lucy."

She took my hand and squeezed it, before reaching up to straighten my crooked collar.

"I can't have you going to my first coronation looking so unkempt," she said, though her eyes were dancing. "Where's Cass, anyway? I thought she would be waiting for us."

As if summoned by the sound of her name, Cass skidded into view, buttoning her jacket up as she went. "I'm ready!"

"I wondered if you were joining us, cousin," Lucy said.

"What, and pass up the chance to witness the coronation of the bastard son? The mysterious King Bravadik? I wouldn't miss this for the world," Cass shot back with a grin.

She sounded a bit out of breath. I gave her a onceover, telegraphing my disapproval. "First my wife, now my cousin? Am I the only one who wants to be on time for this thing?"

Lucy and Cass shared a smirk.

Cass elbowed me in the ribs, none too gently. "*Definitely*, cousin."

"What do you think he's like, anyway?" Lucy leaned close, her fair head beside Cass's dark one. "I've heard rumors he didn't even know his true parentage. It must be a shock to the system, becoming a king when you're not expecting it. Maybe I should have a chat with him. I became a queen by surprise, after all."

"I've heard so many things, they can't possibly all be true," Cass replied.

"Maybe he'll be handsome." Lucy's eyes twinkled playfully. "How would you like a crown of your own, Cass?"

Cass scoffed and rolled her eyes, although a slight flush settled on her cheeks.

"I guess we'll have to wait and see." She clapped her hands together. "Now, let's get a move on. You're going to make us late, Stavrok!"

Ignoring my splutter of indignation, she slid her arm through Lucy's. They strode out of the front doors together into the bright sunshine, leaving me to trail in their wake.

A wide grin had lodged itself firmly onto my face, quite against my will. I couldn't shake it off all the way down the long, winding drive to the castle gates, where the carriages were waiting for us.

THE END

~

~

You can DOWNLOAD book 2, **A King for the Sorceress**, here:
https://books2read.com/u/b5XJE7

Or read on for a sneak peek!

~

CHAPTER
ONE

ERIK

I knelt with my head bowed, every word the elder spoke placing the weight of the world on my shoulders.

"Bravadik Arman. Son of Sigmus, King of the Black Mountains. I anoint you and bestow upon you the kingdom and clan of your father. In your hands, I place responsibility, duty, and power. May this crown grow into a symbol of your strength. May you rise to be the leader your blood rite destines you to become."

I suppressed the shudder that passed through me. I'd dreaded this moment since the day my mother told me the name of my true sire. He had been the last person in the kingdom I expected. *The king.*

"Arise, King Bravadik," the elder said, startling me out of my reflections. I took a long deep breath before pushing to my feet and turning to address the room full of courtiers and honored guests, people who had travelled for the coronation ceremony of the new king.

Cheers and applause rang through the room. The guests were on their feet, shouting for me. Praising me. They were all people I'd never seen before. People I didn't know.

My mother was gone. She had died the past winter, having been ill for many years.

Pain squeezed my chest as though someone had reached inside my ribs and grasped hold of my heart. If I tried, I could picture her standing in the crowd, looking up at me, her eyes shining with devotion and love. She would have been so proud to see me take the throne.

Despite the fact I'd never wanted it.

I still didn't. Not the throne, not the castle. And especially not the kingdom.

Hordes of well-wishers surged forward to congratulate me, and I stumbled down the steps, clasping hands with the first man to step up.

"King Bravadik, it is an honor," he said, smiling broadly. He had a kind, open face, and I couldn't help but smile back.

I made my way through the crowd, greeting people here and there as they waved to me. Relief and disappointment surged through me when I realized that my half-brother's queen wasn't here.

Queen Marienne.

Five years ago, I laid eyes on her for the first time.

The first, and the last.

The crowds before me parted, and a man emerged. With one look, I straightened my spine and lifted my chin to look him in the eye. All of my dragon shifter kinsmen were tall and broad, but there was no mistaking this man for a mere courtier.

"Your Highness," I said, bowing my head.

The man's laugh rolled through his chest, coming out deep and loud. "You're a king now. You bow to no-one."

He reached out, offering me his hand. I recognized the strength in his grip for the test that it was, and squeezed back, hard.

"Thank you for coming," I said.

He grinned at me and pulled the woman next to him closer. Her breasts were so big and round they were practically toppling over the edge of her bodice.

"I'm Stavrok, King of Bravdok." His grin widened. "And this is my wife, Queen Lucy."

"Lucy?" I asked, repeating the strange name.

She smiled, and her whole face lit up. "I'm not from around here."

My gaze slid back to Stavrok and I raised an eyebrow in question.

"I stole her." Stavrok grinned mischievously. "Out of the local village."

"The local... human village?" I repeated, shocked by how casual they sounded.

"Yes," he said, puffing out his chest. "She'd never seen a dragon before."

Lucy rolled her eyes at him, her expression fond. "It's very nice to meet you, Bravadik."

I cringed at the sound of my formal name. "My friends call me Erik."

Stavrok lifted his chin. A smirk tugged at his lips. "You have some of your father in you."

I took a step closer. "You knew him?"

Stavrok nodded. "Very well. Come to our castle for dinner one evening and we will discuss it at length. I've got plenty of old stories."

"I would appreciate that," I said, though my throat clogged with a familiar and overwhelming emotion. "Thank you."

"Come tomorrow night," Lucy said. "Bring Marienne with you. It has been too long since we've seen her. How is she?"

I made some low sound, deep in the back of my throat, and my dragon surged within my chest.

The mood shifted. Stavrok grabbed his wife and shoved her

behind him, all the while rumbling out a growl that made my hackles rise and every muscle in my body clench to keep from shifting then and there.

What the hell?

My dragon was ferocious, sure. But my control was better than *this*.

"Get yourself together, or you're gonna force me to shift," Stavrok hissed through gritted teeth.

I caught a glimpse of his dragon in the way his nostrils flared, and the fire that burned in the depths of his gaze.

I clenched my fists until the knuckles whitened, trying to regain control.

Stavrok summoned a nearby male servant, who snapped to attention.

"A large glass of whiskey for King Bravadik. Now."

The servant dashed away. I forced myself to keep breathing in deep, even inhales and exhales.

Stavrok held Lucy back. The gorgeous little human fought against his arms, resolutely trying to peek around his barrel-like chest to get a look at me.

When the servant reappeared with the glass and a bottle, I downed the first one he poured. The whiskey burned my throat, all the way to my gut.

I demanded another.

I threw back the second one, and when that too reached my empty stomach, the shaking began to subside.

My vision cleared and I could feel my shifter relaxing, yawning, and curling up to sleep inside me.

Stupid thing. We're trying to make a good impression, and you almost started a fight with our neighboring kingdom!

My anger must have shown on my face, because the servant took a couple of steps back like I was going to take a swing any moment.

"Thank you," I said belatedly.

The servant continued to stare at me with startled, wide eyes, not looking reassured in the slightest.

"Please, just..." I grabbed the bottle and waved him off weakly. "Just go."

I looked over at Stavrok, who allowed his little wife back around his huge body so that she could stare up at me with barely disguised curiosity.

"Did I say something wrong?" Lucy asked, then bit her lip in the sweetest way. "I'm still not sure about all the customs... Forgive me if I offended you."

I was too embarrassed to even *look* at her.

I met Stavrok's gaze instead and inclined my head. "Thank you. That drink helped a lot."

Stavrok reached out and squeezed my shoulder. "We need to have that dinner sooner rather than later. Come tomorrow night, with or without Marienne. No arguments."

"But..." Lucy began.

Stavrok gripped her hand and shook his head. "You did nothing wrong, my love. But Marienne is the childless widow of the old king. She will not have a role in this kingdom unless the new king wishes it." His eyes found mine, narrowing. "If I were in his shoes, I would build a house somewhere at the edge of town and put her in it."

Stavrok's gaze intensified. I nodded and hummed as though agreeing.

I could see his point. Marienne was part of the old court, the old ways. Her presence might divide loyalties.

Yes, sending her away would be the logical thing to do.

But the idea didn't sit right with me for a number of reasons, none of which, unfortunately, I could share in my present company.

"Where *is* Marienne, by the way?" Lucy asked as she glanced around, scanning the crowd as if the woman might appear at any moment. "You haven't shipped her off already, have you?"

I shook my head and lifted the bottle of whiskey, taking another sip to calm the way my frame was going rigid again.

"No." I looked down into the bottle, swirling around the liquid inside to avoid her gaze. "I wouldn't do such a thing."

"In that case..." Lucy's glare burned into the side of my head. I could feel it. "Where *is* she?"

I looked over at Stavrok for support. "I would have assumed a human woman would be more malleable..."

Stavrok's laughter was so loud, most of the people in the throne room turned to stare at us.

Lucy whacked him, and he calmed down a little, though nothing could pull the grin from his lips.

"No. Lucy is all fire." He looked down at her with pride. "Especially since giving birth to our triplets. She is the perfect mother dragon for my heirs."

"Triplets?" I repeated.

Wow.

My regard for the little human went up even more. Beauty, brains, and breeding. Stavrok had hit the perfect trifecta.

"Babies, Stavrok. We've talked about this. They are not... heirs." Lucy rolled her eyes.

"Our son *will* inherit the kingdom one day, my love."

I glanced between them with amusement. So, there seemed to be *some* cultural adjustments necessary when it came to human-dragon relationships.

Lucy huffed and puffed, apparently not having an argument for that one. Then, she turned that icy stare back on me. "You didn't answer my question. Where's Marienne?"

I let out a deep sigh.

"I don't know. When I arrived, the staff said she was in mourning and would not be attending my coronation. So..." I turned away from them a little, pretending intense interest in a nearby marble column. "I've left her alone. But I have to assume that she's in the castle somewhere. Hiding."

I neglected to mention that I was hiding from *her,* as well. Nothing would have stopped me from chasing her down if I'd wanted to know where she was.

"Maybe she's in the dungeons," Lucy said under her breath, casting a sidelong look at her husband.

Did she just say *dungeon?* "Why would the queen be in the dungeons?"

Stavrok shook his head. "That's a long story, my friend. We'll have to tell it to you some other time."

He glanced over his shoulder, at the line of people waiting for me. I suppressed a sigh.

"We will see you tomorrow night, Erik," Stavrok said. "Eight o'clock. Bring your appetite."

I shook the king's hand again. This time, his grip seemed friendlier.

"Thank you again for your help." I lifted the bottle to indicate the alcohol, giving him a sheepish smile. My head was slightly buzzing, and my stomach burned with liquor. "I apologize if my behavior scared you, or your lovely wife."

Stavrok chortled, a growly laugh that set my dragon on edge. "Erik, the only reason I didn't take your damn head off was because you obviously don't have much experience controlling your emotions. That has to change, and I'll be happy to help."

I gave the king a smile, trying to remain calm. Rumor was that Stavrok killed my half-brother in hand-to-hand combat. He was a tough warrior. Not one to cross, that was for sure.

"No hard feelings, then?" I asked.

As the king, I needed allies. And, despite his ferocity and loud, bombastic manner, I sensed that Stavrok had a good heart underneath it all.

Stavrok grinned. "As long as you stop staring at my wife's breasts... we're all good."

"Oh... of course." I stammered. Just the first of many royal fuck-ups.

How many would I have before my time was done?

～

You can DOWNLOAD book 2 here:
https://books2read.com/u/b5XJE7